T0375512

CONVERSATIONS

CONVERSATIONS

Donald Krist

Copyright © 2007 by Donald Krist.

ISBN: Hardcover   978-1-4257-5887-5
                Softcover   978-1-4257-5850-9

All rights reserved. No part of this book may be reproduced or transmitted
in any form or by any means, electronic or mechanical, including photocopying,
recording, or by any information storage and retrieval system,
without permission in writing from the copyright owner.

This is a work of fiction. Names, characters, places and incidents either are the product
of the author's imagination or are used fictitiously, and any resemblance to any actual
persons, living or dead, events, or locales is entirely coincidental.

This book was printed in the United States of America.

To order additional copies of this book, contact:
Xlibris Corporation
1-888-795-4274
www.Xlibris.com
Orders@Xlibris.com
39431

CONTENTS

CHAPTER I   Dinners at Jackie's and Younkers Tearoom 9
CHAPTER II   Look at Her Like a Fabergé 14
CHAPTER III   Dinner at Julie's 18
CHAPTER IV   Dinner at Tiffany's 23
CHAPTER V   Dinner at Margaret's 28
CHAPTER VI   Dinner at Marilyn's 33
CHAPTER VII   Dinner at Mollie's 38
CHAPTER VIII   Dinner at Rosemary's 43
CHAPTER IX   Dinner at Katie's 48
CHAPTER X   Picnic Dinner at Norma's 53
CHAPTER XI   Dinner at Rosie's 59
CHAPTER XII   Dinner at Leyria's 65
CHAPTER XIII   Dating After Sixty 69
CHAPTER XIV   Dinner at Wang Ho's Marilyn is Ailing 72
CHAPTER XV   Dinner at Jackie's Marilyn's Diagnosis Confirmed 77
CHAPTER XVI   Marilyn's Journey Home 83

PROLOGUE

Tiffany is a stunning blonde beauty of twenty with an ambience about her that radiates like fine crystal.

Her tall, lithe body is firm and curved, with shapely overtones transmitting sexual voltage, forcing people instinctively to stare as she passes.

And her skin actually reflects light, much like that renaissance painters brushed onto the cherubs of their canvas.

But it is her expressive, dancing eyes that really strike you as you first begin to detail this beautiful apparition piece by piece from the top down. They glow a deep phosphorescent blue, like Lake Zurich at dusk.

Under wide-arched eyebrows, these appealing orbs with slightly slanted lids give her face an almost Oriental mysticism that attracts and hangs on as if you are gazing into the shadows of a haunted ancient garden by moonlight.

And Tiffany has a voice to match all this: low, cool, silken and smooth as it strokes your senses with its charm and carefully chosen enunciations, each utterance seeming to speak with a secret all its own.

Tiffany, remarkably, has absolutely no affectations. She is truly almost shy and never lets on she is one of those girls born to rare beauty. She is a lovely, classy first edition, put together with all the binder's art, like a family Bible.

With the poise of a trained actress, she moves to unheard music. And when she flashes her gorgeous smile, it is for you alone.

You could guess that she has been raised with money, lots of it—in the quaint, half-million dollar cottages of Martha's Vineyard, not far from the legendary "Black Dog Tavern" landmark, where nearby multi-million dollar yachts loll at anchor in quiet dignity.

Tiffany knew mansions on Long Island. She had enrolled at Vassar but dropped out after a year.

Now she is a beautiful, just-retired prostitute with a short, spotty, dark past, eager to get on with her young life.

What happened?

CHAPTER I

DINNERS AT JACKIE'S AND YOUNKERS TEAROOM

Members of the Pickle Club wanted to know. And they also are curious as to how the hell Tiffany got into their exclusive club.

"Well, I guess I'm the culprit," acknowledged Jackie to the group, all gathered at her house in West Des Moines that cold, snowy, early December evening.

"I invited her into our group, knowing about her past . . ."

"Do you think we really want her to meet with us? On a regular basis?" questioned Marilyn, one of the founders of the Pickle Club.

"We all knew about her via the grapevine after our last meeting when she showed up and didn't say much, and you said you'd invited her," Marilyn continued. "We were all astounded by her beauty and bearing, but . . . have you since thought about the ramifications when our husbands, children, friends and business associates find out she was a high-priced call girl in New York? And we've taken her in?" Marilyn added.

"Well, yes, I have," Jackie answered with muted defiance, her shoulders back . . . "I think she deserves our sympathy and understanding. She's trying to make a new life for herself here. She called me this afternoon telling me she had a cold and wouldn't be here tonight. This is probably a good time to hash this out and whether we want to give her a new member pickle Christmas tree ornament as a sign of our acceptance.

"You all decide. But let me tell you the story as she told it to me . . ."

The snow outside thickened, and a mounting north wind blew crystallizing flakes against the windows of Jackie's condominium with a brassy resonance.

"She moved in here near me late last fall," Jackie began. "She bought the last condo for sale down the street. I noticed the furniture trucks first. She bought all new stuff. And, as they took it in, I saw it was beautiful—and massive; traditional white with some Empire, some Italian. Lots of white leather.

"I saw her briefly in and out when she moved in and then when she walked her dog. A beautiful tan Lab. She'd go past my condo and I could see she was a beauty.

"Now, I know most of the people in the area. Block parties, open houses and stuff. So I couldn't wait to meet Tiffany.

"So one day I managed to bump into her as I was getting my mail. I complimented her on her choice of dogs but asked if she knew about the Lab's tendency for developing bad hip bones.

"She smiled and said, 'Oh, yes. I know about that because we've had them at home in New York and always took them to our summer cottage at Martha's Vineyard for a usual swinging, rompin' good time. They've bred that hip weakness out of most registered Labs now. Besides, I give my Charlie calcium and other vitamins for good bone structure.'

"Well, we ended up sitting on my condo porch for a good part of that afternoon. I knew she was very lonely. It was pretty obvious she didn't know anyone here. Seemed to be just glad to have someone to talk to. I told her I'd have a coffee and introduce her to my neighborhood friends for starters, and perhaps she'd like to join our Pickle Club . . ."

"You invited her to join us before you knew about her background?" asked an anxious Angie.

"Yes, I did. But let me finish . . . So I had her come to my house for a couple of coffees with my neighbor friends . . . She didn't say much then either. In the meantime, I asked her over for coffee, just she and me. Trying to get conversation out of her privately, I learned more about her, but it was like pulling teeth.

"She had grown up as an only child on Long Island in a very wealthy family atmosphere. Chauffeured by limousine to private schools in Long Island and Queens. Even private tutors. She said she was always very lonely. And that her parents told her she was a slow learner. Because of her solitude.

"Perhaps really because her mother was an alcoholic and her financier father was never home. When he was, she said, tears in her eyes, her mother and father fought ferociously, especially over the mistress her father kept in an apartment in Manhattan.

"They never divorced, she said, because of Tiffany. Mostly her mother's sentiments, 'cause she said she didn't think her father really gave a damn about her . . .

"So, with these distractions, I knew she grew up timid and afraid.

"And she told me she had 'a lot of piano lessons 'cause they took up a lot of time with practicing and all,'" Jackie added.

"But she was a startling beauty, I guess, from the time she was 14 or 15, from what she said of her parents' comments. She showed me pictures taken at that time, and she really was an early beauty.

"So her first year at Vassar, she'd just started, she said. Totally unworldly and inexperienced in just about everything, she met this guy. There were plenty of them around, making passes at the Vassar girls all the time . . ."

The attentive Pickle Club members had the spell of continuity briefly broken by Jackie standing up and refilling their glasses. She sat down and continued after a long sip from her glass.

"And this guy wanted her to come across. She'd had a few inconsequential dates. But she had no idea what this guy was trying to do. So she pushed him away in confusion and bewilderment because she had no clue what all was involved here.

"She told me this was a totally new experience, and it was hard for her to tell me this. She was embarrassed.

"'I grew up kind of shy, I guess,' she said. 'I knew this wasn't right.'

"Anyway, fighting back tears which were now flowing, she said the guy just drew back and left. But he called her later in the week, apologized and made another date with her.

"She says she should have never gone out with him again, because she knew he was going to make another try. After all, she said tearfully, he was a handsome athlete, and as a jock, she said, he had a lot of friends.

"To make a long story short, she didn't know he was dropping meth into the drink she was nursing until she really didn't know what was going on. And she said this is how a lot of girls get hooked on this highly addictive drug . . . Guys just can't wait to get it done, so they pill or powder you to death. And she said that's what happened to her.

"She said meth is so addictive, it just takes one dose and you're hooked. So this guy had his way with her many times, because she was a virgin, and he seemed to like that. And he gave her more meth.

"But after a few months, he dumped her."

"What then?" Molly asked. "He must have been doping her up all those months . . ."

"Yup, and she was really hooked. Her studies were a total mess. Even her dysfunctional parents noticed the change in her.

"But she found a new source for meth in Queens. And for cocaine. She was now into it but had to finance her addiction. She had a trust fund her grandfather had set up for her, but she couldn't get to that until she was 21.

"So she—and believe me, it was awful hard for her to tell me this—hooked up with a call-girl madam in Manhattan.

"She had a little money, so she moved out of the family mansion in Long Island and got an apartment in downtown Manhattan. She became a call girl for only the top clients on her madam's list, to support her growing habit: doctors, lawyers, judges, finance people, people in show business, on a very selective basis and for only a short time, she said, because she couldn't stand some of the kinky stuff they would want her to do. She said she told the madam that she, with her beauty, felt she didn't have to do anything but the missionary position stuff, and with a condom every time.

"After a short while, the clients told her boss they were dissatisfied and quit calling the agency. Tiffany said she told her, "The hell with this," and quit after only a few weeks. She said in desperation she got a lawyer to get at her trust fund, and split the two million dollars with him, because he had to pay off a judge to get it done . . ."

"Why didn't she ask one of the judges she was screwing?" asked Angie.

"Probably she didn't want any of her clients to know her real name."

"And what *is* her last name?" queried Rosemary.

"Vander Waal, one of the oldest and most prestigious families in New York," Jackie answered.

"She must really trust you to be telling you all this," Rosie interjected. "But why should she?"

"Because I sympathized with her and told her so. I also told her I thought we'd all help her . . ."

"Is she still on dope?" quizzed Leyria.

"No. She got into detox and treatment in Arizona and told her parents she wanted to get away. She told me she really just wanted to get as far away from New York as possible.

"So she looked at locations in an Atlas but chose West Des Moines because she had driven through on the interstate coming back from Arizona to New York to get her stuff."

"And here she is," said Katie. "Did you tell her anything about us as individuals when you asked her to join our little group?"

"Oh, yes. I explained our Pickle Club was a group of 11 women of all ages from 21 to 65, upper middle class, some of us very well-to-do, others just well off, from all walks of life. Married to a grand group of guys who mostly spoil us all. Most of us."

"Hey, wait," mumbled Angie. "I don't feel spoiled. But I'm not even married."

"Well, you know what I mean. None of us have Tiffany's pain and bad memories like she has to try to forget," Jackie said, answering Angie's non-sequiter.

"I told her the group started as a neighborhood coffee club of Marilyn, Rosie and Katie and grew with new members, friends of friends, into the outer reaches of West Des Moines and the other suburbs.

"And I told her we all were very particular who joined our group because we had a waiting list of those who wanted to get in. But more than 11 gals would be too unwieldy to entertain, and we couldn't all eat off of TV trays all the time but at a dining room or kitchen table, like we normally do. Even buffet style, which is what, as you know, we do a lot, too.

"I told her we all at our invitation dinner have told our brief life history and what kind of work we have done or are still doing, and she would have to do the same.

"I told her Marilyn, Katie and Rosie, as founders, were also the group's entertainers most of the time.

"And that sometimes we take brief, out-of-town trips or just talk and cut-up, gossip, and tell stories of our childhood at each others' homes. And sometimes when we run out of chatter, we play cards or other games, or we just eat at a restaurant. But that our meetings are never boring and that *we always really support one another.*

"*One solid rule we all firmly agreed to was: No discussion of religion or politics.*

"Our calling committee of Angie and Mollie handles the phone reminders to everyone with the location and dishes to bring, if needed."

Jackie added, "Tiffany suggested 'Can't I just say I wanted to move out west, away from New York and my family? I have a job at the West Des Moines Library, and I could tell about that, couldn't I? And just let it go at that?'"

"I told her I thought we could gloss over her past, but you all seem to know her background anyway, or at least part of it . . ."

"Yeah. The real estate agent she bought her condo from checked her previous address in downtown Manhattan and found out about her high-class call girl routine. That's how we found out. I got a call from Katie."

"And the rest is gossip history. Right?" Jackie almost snarled.

CHAPTER II

LOOK AT HER LIKE A FABERGÉ

"I have my doubts about whether Tiffany would really add much to our group," said Marilyn, who seldom, if ever, stated a negative to the group, or about anyone.

But Marilyn knew from experience that when you state the negative first, then go to a positive, you can to make a turnabout in any argument.

"But I for one am willing to give her a try, on a provisional basis . . . See what the rest of you think . . . Wanta give her a chance?

"Look at her kind of like a fabergé egg. You know, exquisitely beautiful on the outside but empty inside," Marilyn explained, taking a deep breath of resignation.

"I think we can help her a lot . . . especially with all of us guys drawing her out and kidding her . . . ," Marilyn added. "We can fill 'er in."

"What the hell is a fabergé egg?" challenged Mollie.

"It's a perfume, isn't it?" volunteered Angie, crinkling her nose.

"Oh, God, you young smucks," snapped Rosemary. "Carl Fabergé was the crown jeweler to the czars in Russia. He designed the first fabergé egg for Alexander III as an Easter gift for his wife Maria, and Czar Nicholas II decided he wanted to continue giving them as special gifts . . ."

"Now, would you listen to our court historian," breathed Katie.

"Yeah, and one of the first ones Nicholas issued was as a commemorative for the opening of the Trans-Siberian Railroad," retorted Rosemary. "I know about 'em, 'cause I picked up a cheap copy of one at a garage sale and read up on them. The publisher Malcolm Forbes collected several million dollars worth of the originals. So there . . ."

"Anyway," Jackie added emphatically," let's give this beautiful girl a chance. I'll second Marilyn's motion we take her in."

Jackie glanced around the room at most of the heads nodding in tacit approval.

If Marilyn recommended it, it must be all right.

"And I don't think we need to bring up the whore angle at all," Marilyn suggested. "After all, she wasn't just any ol' street walker," she added with a half-wry smile. "She *was* selective."

"I think we should just think of her as wanting to get away on her own, away from New York, and landing a job in the West Des Moines Library on her way back from a therapy session in Arizona after an unfortunate experience at Vassar. Okay?" suggested Jackie, half pleadingly.

"Now, how about our Christmas party with husbands?" she quietly added. "Where shall we go?" Jackie paused, glancing around at the faces in the room. "Think about it while we eat, maybe. Let's adjourn to the table, and I'll serve up my hot soufflé special with ham. Okay?" she ordered, nodding toward her dining room table. "Make your pit stops now if you want. You all know where the bathrooms are . . ."

Jackie's condominium was new with white, clean, airy bathrooms on two levels. All new, heavy, modern, white wood and tapestry furniture graced the place with Utrillo and Modigliani reproduction paintings in the front rooms and hallway, and other tasteful art elsewhere.

Members of the Pickle Club were amazed when she and Bill acquired the new property and furniture, because their house at the time near Rosie, Marilyn and Katie, although a modern contemporary, had been poorly furnished.

Then Jackie and Bill lost their home to repossession when Bill's early-on Alzheimer's began affecting his work as sales manager for one of the leading car dealers in West Des Moines. He lost his job. Bill, a former handsome Marine veteran of the Korean War, was soon reduced to odd jobs and began a steady diet of Aricept and Memantine pills to slow down the disease. He could no longer even drive a car. Jackie had to get him to and from work on her schedule as a child daycare center manager. Their daughter by now had married and left home and was so engrossed in her life with a new husband that she was of little help to Bill and Jackie. So the pair languished in apartment rentals. But Jackie still kept her membership active in the Pickle Club, to keep her sanity, she often said.

The Pickle Club was called "The Therapy Group" by Marilyn ("'cause we all feel better afterward," she said). It gave Bill and Jackie all the support they could, as they did to the spouses and children of deceased Pickle Club members Nancy and Mary when they passed away from breast cancer and myasthenia gravis respectively.

They were immediately replaced as members by Mollie and Angie because the older Pickle Club members thought aloud numerous times, "We need younger blood, new life."

"Will they entertain us with their worldly knowledge and earthly experience? Probably not," Marilyn observed.

"But they'll surely laugh at our old jokes . . . , and that's really important," she said with a big smile.

The first question Angie posed when asked to join the Pickle Club was, "Why is this group called the 'Pickle Club'? Is it because of a phallic reference? For a group of 'ol ladies? Or what?"

"No," Rosie patiently explained. "Not that at all. Look up 'pickle' in any dictionary. It defines *pickle* as not only a vegetable or a process for preserving foods, but as an awkward, difficult or problematic situation. That's what we're all about.

"We started out talking about our everyday problems and awkward situations, and Marilyn always made them sound so funny, we continued as 'group therapy,' as she calls it.

"So we empathize, cry sometimes, but we laugh a lot," Rosie concluded.

Jackie, with straight black hair, plain, undistinguished facial characteristics and deep brown, almost black eyes, dieted a square figure. But no one noticed. They all liked her friendly interest in them and her willingness to help whenever she could. Jackie's mother had recently died suddenly and left her and her sister each $25,000, making the new condo and furniture possible. It was a godsend, Jackie acknowledged.

Jackie, although admittedly just a plain Jewish lady, prided herself on her cooking. As a matter of fact, she was the gourmet of the group and passed judgment on all things that had been, or could be, cooked.

And now with a new stove and oven, she could try what had been impossible before.

Jackie's table settings, like all in the group, were the best she could muster for the event or occasion. Elaborate table centerpieces, in the season, with the best China, silver and accent pieces—even when a member of the group hosted a buffet meal.

Tonight the centerpiece was a white and silver Christmas tree miniature about 18 inches high, surrounded at the base by a red cherry wreath, sitting on an oval mirror.

Napkin rings were colorful, circular Santas, and the napkins and tablecloth were golden with red and white accents, the cloth covered with a green net spotted with white Christmas trees on each corner.

Sitting down, after serving the group, with help from Katie who almost always pitched in for serving, if needed, and the cleanup afterward, Jackie took a deep breath and acknowledged the "ooh's and ah's" of satisfaction with her cooking.

"Okay. Next thing. Where for our husbands' Christmas party?"

"How about the Younkers Tearoom?" Leyria suggested.

She glanced around at the murmurs and shrugged shoulders and added, "Most of us have been there for Christmas buffets, bridal luncheons, first dates, or tea with Grandma . . . How 'bout it? . . ."

"Fine with me," said Marilyn.

"They're goin' to close the Younkers Department Store next summer, so it will be our last chance probably ever to go there again," joined in Norma, eyeing the consensus around the table.

"I'll make the arrangements," said Leyria. "I think we can get a nice buffet for about eight bucks a person, and I'll have them reserve three tables for eight each. If we can get in."

"Fine," Rosemary agreed. "Let's draw gift names now. And that'll be a nice party for our husbands to see and meet Tiffany," she added, surveying the group as Jackie rose to begin packing oatmeal and chocolate chip cookies and date bars for delivery to the husband of the month, as Pickle Club custom dictated. Each month different lucky husbands were rotated to receive this treat by the hostess.

"And the Christmas party at the Younkers Tearoom should be good neutral ground to introduce this beautiful Tiffany whore person to the husbands and at the same time keep her at bay for a while," thought Rosemary. *"Thank God I don't have a husband to worry about . . . We'll see what happens."*

Rosemary and a couple others in the Pickle Club had little to worry about. The Christmas party at Younkers Tearoom a week before Christmas was a resounding success with a good buffet of roast beef and mashed potatoes, gravy and green beans, with sherbet. And a talented harpist soothed the Pickle Club diners, and others filling the tearoom, with Christmas carols as they ate and then distributed their gifts in a quiet and orderly fashion.

Then in a quiet ceremony for Tiffany, the group had her stand to be introduced officially to the husbands, and inducted her into the Pickle Club by presenting her with the green pickle Christmas tree ornament. Tiffany fit in quite well, drew a lot of attention from the husbands, and left, as she had arrived, with Jackie and Bill.

Just before leaving, the group decided the January meeting would be held at Julie's home, so they could discuss the holiday movies, good and bad.

Upon leaving, they all ogled the legendary Younkers Tearoom for the last time: the plush carpets, draperies, formal chandeliers, classic molded white pillars against red-draped walls, and the white-on-white tablecloth. The tearoom classic, the Bit Burger, part of the buffet offering, settled well in a number of full stomachs.

CHAPTER III

DINNER AT JULIE'S

"We did see a number of good movies over the holidays," volunteered Rosie to the January Pickle Club group gathered in Julie's new home in south Des Moines.

"'Cold Mountain' certainly should win a 2004 Academy Award for Nicole Kidman. It's such a physical departure for her in this picture. She's so pretty in real life, and sooo ugly in this movie. And maybe one for Renee Zellwager, too, for that matter," Rosie emphasized.

"Right," observed Mollie, "and the same is true for Charlize Theron in 'Monster.' She's almost hideous to look at in this movie but does a great job of acting . . ."

"The one that stood out for me was the 'Girl With the Pearl Earring,'" announced Margaret. "Somewhat the true story of Vermeer with some great acting by Scarlett Johansson. She really is a beauty and plays this part to perfection."

"What about 'Lord of the Rings,' 'Return of the King?'" retorted Tiffany. Mollie and Angie both nodded in hearty agreement. To all in the younger age group, this picture notably appealed to them.

"Excellent, as was the 'The Last Samurai' and 'Mona Lisa's Smile,' 'Peter Pan' and 'The House of Sand and Fog,'" Tiffany added.

"You must go to a lot of movies," declared Rosemary with an edge on her voice.

"Yes, I have been," retorted Tiffany, "but I'm so grateful to all of you for making me a member of your Pickle Club," Tiffany chirped, taking the edge off Rosemary's comment. "So I don't have to look for my entertainment in just movie houses," Tiffany summed up.

"We do want you to feel at home," said Jackie warmly, standing to pour wine into a tray full of glasses, then setting out some bowls of cashews and mixed nuts.

"Well, I'm also grateful to Mollie and Angie for asking me to go with them for most of those I got to see over the holidays," Tiffany said shyly.

Tonight's Pickle Club hostess Julie, a very attractive, outgoing, slim brunette, as General Manager of the Fleur Cinema and Café, was rising in her career. Although still quite young (24), she was now responsible for a major Des Moines theater group with four screens and stand-up table and seating capacities for the café in the lobbies of the theaters. And she was well paid for its success.

Born on a farm near Danbury, a small hamlet in western Iowa, she grew up attending Catholic schools and was active in 4-H Club farm youth work. She was named Iowa State Fair Queen after heavy competition in 1993 and traveled the state with her mother as chaperone for nearly a year, making appearances at Iowa's county fairs and corndog festivals.

She then enrolled at Iowa State University and pledged Delta Zeta sorority, majoring in psychology and learning education, aiming at a child counseling job after graduation.

Which is just what she did. Her first job upon graduation was as a treatment counselor for child disorders at Orchard Place in Des Moines, a campus of daycare cottages for youngsters 13 to 18, many sexually abused with schizoid and polar disorders.

"We treatment counselors were basically the parents most of these kids never had," Julie told the Pickle Club one night. We did basic interviews and legwork for staff and retained psychiatrists and then sat in on their series of treatment interviews as they prescribed a lot of Proacterin, Librium, Valium, Prozac, and other stuff. You would not believe some of the things I saw and heard during those years," Julie emphasized.

"Some of these kids were forced to have sex while their parents watched. Others watched as their drugged parents did a lot of very strange things. One twelve-year-old maintained an uncontrolled anger complex, always beating up on the kids around him. He finally was put in isolation after he broke the back of an eleven-year-old girl. This boy came from a family of five kids, all with different fathers.

"We had to counsel these kids that whatever had happened, it was not their fault. We really seemed to be the parents they never had recognized.

"I liked the work I was doing for some four years, but then I had some misfortune of my own that caused me to retire for a year. I lost my older sisters, Marlys and Cheryl, bang, bang—just like that, one in a car wreck, the other in a small plane crash, only three weeks apart.

"Let me tell you guys, I had to fall back and regroup and contemplate the future.

"Then when my father died, I think of a broken heart, a short time later, I had to stay close to Mother. She was falling apart . . .

"This was all a real wakeup call for me."

In the meantime, Julie said, she was dating her present husband whom she had met while at Iowa State University. "I think at the time he was the only reason I kept going. My parents didn't like him when I took him home with me one holiday season. I told them I had met him at a fraternity open house. He drank a lot and played the guitar all the time.

"Well, honestly, I thought he was sort of a dork at first, but I kinda got to like him, especially at those critical periods in my life. We married after I got pregnant and had our daughter. Tim dropped out of college and went on the road, playing lead guitar and singing with his rock group.

"They've just recorded their first album, so we think he may be on the way.

"Meanwhile some friends introduced me at a party to the owner of the Fleur Cinema and Café, and he hired me on the spot as the general manager on a trial basis.

"'Build it up' was all he said. 'You're in total charge.'"

"So you have certainly, from all indications," Margaret observed, being well conversant with management problems.

"I like to think so," Julie answered.

"It's my first management job, and I really enjoy supervising the employees, concessions and menus, doing the advertising and promotion, booking movies and so forth. We have some 22 employees who are a most interesting group of young ladies, even younger than me. I have to keep an eye on their hair dye jobs, body rings and tattoo exposures, though . . ."

"We've all been out to your theaters, and they are very nice. Cleanest lobby, restrooms and seating areas of any theaters in town. But, frankly, some of the pictures you exhibit suck," Rosemary snorted. "Do you personally choose them?"

"You're partially right. Some of them *are* pretty bad. I only pick the ones of those I get offered. Our booking agent in Los Angeles calls me every Monday with a selected menu for me to choose from. He works only with independent theaters and schedules pictures mostly that have done well at film festivals, like the Venice, Toronto, Stockholm, Cannes, Sundance, and Tribeca film festivals, for example. We get our advance promo film trailers about three weeks, sometimes five weeks out . . ."

"Well, the ones I've seen out there have a lot of subtitles," said Rosie.

"You're right," said Julie, "but we also get real classics like the recent 'The March of the Penguins' narrated by Morgan Freeman and 'Ladies in Lavender' with Judy Dench and some others."

"That's right," volunteered Marilyn, always taking a positive approach. "We've seen some pretty good ones at your theaters. Take 'Ladies in Lavender.' There was some really great sound stage music as well as the work of the violinist, Joshua Bell, who did the soundtrack for the actor violinist in the picture.

"As you all know, hubby Don's father was a violin prodigy and conductor. I just wish he could have seen this picture. Really better than the old Intermezzo, and José Iturbi musical movies . . ."

"Well," said Julie, a slight frown of concern crossing her face. "The deaths of my loved ones made me appreciate what they did for me and what I have left. What my parents went through in raising three daughters and then losing two of them. And then my dad trying to hold it together farming 2500 acres of oats, corn, pigs, and cattle. And then, bang. Makes me pause and reflect on what life's all about . . .

"Mom's selling the farm now, and will probably move here. To baby-sit my daughter, I hope. At least some of the time, like she is tonight . . ."

"Let's eat," said Julie, rising and shaking away her unpleasant memories, with still shadows of a dim look at the future.

"It'll all work out," said Marilyn cheerfully, rising to join the others.

"I hope you enjoy your Italian sausage pizza with Italian bread, Vienna butter, and tossed Italian salad on the buffet. I've added Italian manicotti as a side dish for you all. And a different Rosét wine. Hope you like it. Had it all brought in from the theaters. It's what we serve there, as some of you know.

"If you don't like pizza," she added, "I have some cavatelli pasta and shrimp Alfredo, as you'll see. If you don't like the manicotti, try the chicken carbonara or the pasta primonera."

"Gourmet," Jackie moaned loudly in feigned appreciation and anticipation. "There goes another three pounds," she breathed.

"And especially for Tiffany, try the New York cheesecake for dessert," Julie added.

"Easy way to play hostess," thought Rosemary.

"Cheap way to entertain," mused Angie.

"Gee, I haven't had pizza for a long time. Good idea," mused Marilyn meditatively aloud, always upbeat.

"You have such a lovely house. You've really done well decorating it," Tiffany observed, standing. "I like your cozy Early American maple and your colonial art—portrait oils and scenes on barnboard. It's all so comfortable and nice . . ." she continued.

"Well, I'm sure you've seen much nicer in your mansion on Long Island. Probably a richly textured, black, clubby leather affluence maybe."

"Yes," said Tiffany, mouthing her words carefully. *"But this is home."*

*   *   *

After appropriately stuffing themselves at Julie's buffet, the Pickle Club members drew charades characters on an art easel and played bunco on three boards. And, after a short bingo game, noisily enjoyed Marilyn's jokes, Katie's response and repartee, and Angie's deliberately stupid and prodding questions after Marilyn's joke—like, "And how much would you like to contribute to the Indian Relief Fund, Mrs. Custer?"

"Who was Custer? . . ." asked Angie in feigned ignorance.

"Okay, you guys. Where do we go next?" asked Molly.

"I'd like to hostess the next month's meeting of the Pickle Club," volunteered Tiffany. There was no doubt in anybody's mind that they all agreed. Was it curiosity? Envy? Comparison decorating?

CHAPTER IV

DINNER AT TIFFANY'S

All of the above.

"I've just been dying to see your new place," gushed Norma upon entering Tiffany's new condo.

"Why, it's just gorgeous!" she exclaimed, taking off her coat, handing it to Tiffany and glancing around.

Indeed, members of the Pickle Club that night were all amazed at the beauty, good taste and thoughtfulness that Tiffany had demonstrated throughout her home.

The basic style throughout the condominium was heavy, white, traditional wood and leather furnishings with Louis XIV, Empire and Victorian overtones. Throw pillows of muted colors and cotton textures, occasional tables to match the chairs and sofas. Tapestries and other tasteful art-museum-caliber; sculptures of Greek and Roman vintage, with some moderns, some real artifacts, others just good copies, added to a mixture of oil paintings of modern and Aztec art, with Degas and Renoir copies in oil. A couple groupings of muted Cézanne's watercolor flower garden scenes, with large sea and landscape scenes in elaborate frames, had been thoughtfully placed here and there.

But it was her stunning use of color—dark red, gray and muted brown walls contrasting white woodwork and white and gray art objects on pedestals in front of them—that drew ooh's and ah's, as well as the Lladro and Daun porcelains and Lalique crystal pieces scattered here and there.

What especially interested everybody was the white Steinway grand piano in an alcove off the living room. Surprisingly, Tiffany acknowledged their gathering and staring at the Steinway by saying, "Yes, I'll play for you after dinner," Tiffany promised the gathered group. "Meanwhile, the bar's open," she said, pointing to a white-jacketed Korean bar boy, friend of Katie's, standing in the back of the room.

"I'm not showing off," Tiffany apologized. "I just don't know how to mix drinks, and after you've all been drinking wine for so many of your meetings, I thought you might like to order mixed drinks of your choice . . ."

"Yeah," muttered Angie. "We can really get plastered tonight."

"Well, to get you started, we have margaritas, brown daiquiris, pink ladies, and for you who are adventurous, Devil's tails . . ."

"What the hell are those?" queried an excited Margaret, who prided herself on being a bit sophisticated.

"They're a mix of rum, vodka with lime juice and apricot liquor, and a lime peel. For those of you who need a heavier dose of spirits, I recommend this one . . ."

Half the group ordered Devil's tails just for the adventure, and a smiling Korean bar boy turned to the marble-tiled, all-automatic kitchen, saying to himself, "Powerful stuff. But pleasant." He already had two ice blenders full and ready to go. "But not pugnacious," he added to himself.

"Let's get shit-faced," muttered Margaret, as the drinks were brought out a short time later.

"Now, please tell us what you do at the library," Margaret asked Tiffany, eyeing her Devil's tail, the strange-looking concoction in her upheld hand.

"Well, I do a lot of things," Tiffany answered, with a pensive slight frown. "From checking books in and out, not only regular and large-print books but DVDs, tapes, CDs and children's games, doing reception desk work, giving directions to people wanting section numbers to look for books, along with instructions and additional help to other people on how to use our computers more effectively. I also do phone book renewals for extension.

"You know, after a brief orientation, the Library paid for a 30-day training period for me on computers—so I'm now semi-skilled, I guess," Tiffany added, a pleased smile replacing the frown.

"How have computers especially helped you and the Library?" asked Mollie, who had just completed an advanced computer training course.

"I can't imagine how old-time librarians were able to function without them. Library customers could use card files, of course, but locating book sections and the books, I'm sure, took twice as long as it does now. Think of it. How much easier it is now to catalog and record book titles, descriptions, measurements, copyright dates, and BN numbers. Computers are almost indispensable in ordering book replacement copies—

"I get to order these new books, too . . ."

"How do you pick them?" queried Angie.

"Well, most are pretty heavily advertised in *The Daily Press*, *New York Times* Booksellers' List, *Publishers Weekly*, and *The Library Journal*.

"You may or may not know, the bestseller list used to be based on *the number of books shipped from publishers, not sold*. But I think that's been corrected now in large part.

"I get to handle the telephone information requests, too, when I'm on the reception and information desk," Tiffany continued. "I got a special training course on where to look for different types of information in the various reference books we have on file near the desk. You wouldn't believe what type of things people ask for," Tiffany pointed out.

The group had by now been served their drinks and were all attentively listening to Tiffany's library discourse of things they had never heard or thought of. And she was presenting it all proudly, like a professor in a classroom.

"Like what?" Angie prodded.

"Well, one I got recently was, 'Have you got anything on flying gerbils?' When I get these kinds of questions, I tell them I'll call them back when I've researched the question. I looked and looked in several encyclopedias, animal guides and veterinarian texts, and called the lady back after deciding that flying fish was as close as I could get. I told her there wasn't anything on a flying gerbil. 'Oh,' she said. 'What I really meant was a flying dirigible.'

"Someone else wanted to get some information on the name of Sir Lancelot's horse. Another called to ask, and I found, the number of feathers on the average duck."

"Gaud," breathed Margaret in a huffed exclamation. "This is what we property owners are paying taxes for?"

"Isn't it awful? But it's all necessary because we're a full-service agency of the city . . . What you can't imagine is what we find in returned books . . . ," replied Tiffany.

"Like what?" asked Marilyn.

"Apple cores, movie and theater ticket stubs, gum wrappers, tree leaves, postcards, pieces of mail, envelopes, letters, bills, dental appointment printouts, playing cards—mostly, I'm sure, used as bookmarkers.

"But still I wonder what real use would the couple of wrapped condoms I found in returned books have—" Tiffany questioned after a long sip of her Devil's tail drink.

"You know," Tiffany paused, deliberating her words carefully, remembering the Pickle Club's strict rule against any discussion of religion as well as politics. "I even found religious stuffers in some of the returned books. Like several pamphlets saying, 'You don't need a god to live a good life,' with a card showing an anti-religious group on a website in Iowa City.

"During the past ten months, I've found some fifty religious pamphlets touting Christianity and special beliefs, from Jehovah's Witnesses to Judaism and Buddhism.

"I reported all this to the library director, who said evangelizing by placing unauthorized materials in library books is inappropriate. The returned books in many cases were easily traceable to the library cardholders, and they were sent gentle desist letters . . .

"What was your greatest challenge in your time with the library so far?" asked Marilyn.

Tiffany paused, pondered a moment and took a long sip of her drink and answered, "I guess dealing with people returning damaged books. Most of them are parents whose kids have torn out or cut out their favorite pop-up characters or color illustrations from their checked-out books. Of course, the parents have to pay for the books."

"Did you get in on any of the children's programs last summer?" asked Rosie.

"Oh, yes," answered Tiffany enthusiastically. "I sure did. I'd just finished my training. It was so much fun watching the kids in the West Des Moines Library's special Summer Camp Programs. I monitored some, directed some, and participated in a lot of them.

"We had take-home crafts for the three to six year olds, based on the stories we had just read to them.

"Our new easy-reader books for the slightly older kids are getting so much better, from the awful basics I knew as a child to much more believable and mature themes.

"We have toddler board books with cardboard jump-outs, some with puppets to go with the stories that we could use to entertain the kids."

"Most of these kids are preschoolers, right?" asked Rosie.

"Yes. Most people don't know we've got nearly 20 million preschoolers in our country. I think most of them in West Des Moines, because we always have great crowds of happy, noisy kids during the summer."

"What was the most fun for you during these kids' summer programs?" Marilyn asked again.

"Oh, there were several. I think the doggie wash sessions that we had where the kids washed down dogs brought in from their families. And of course when the kids brought their grandparents—their granny nannies. The main difference between parents and these granny nannies is the lack of time restraint. These grandparents were a big help to us with the rollicking, rolling, fast-moving bunch of kids every day.

"Children learn by doing, as you know, and the hassle with them at times is made all worthwhile by their laughs, smiles and giggles.

"We had to take twice the time to explain things they didn't understand by singing silly songs, telling silly jokes, making faces to make them laugh and understand . . ."

The Pickle Club that night just then saw a much warmer and whimsical side of Tiffany than they had before. Other than the cold, steel-plated reserved beauty, thought Marilyn—and others there. And unlike the fabergé eggs, Tiffany did have an interior—much deeper and warmer than any of them had at first thought.

All the while this animated conversation was going on, Tiffany's Korean bar boy doubled as a barbecue gourmet by frying T-bone steaks on the kitchen grill and adding a tangy Western sauce on them, served with baked potatoes and corn on the cob Tiffany had sent out from the cold-storage vaults of the downtown Des Moines Embassy Club.

All the cooking orders he had carefully and courteously taken beforehand, and he announced he was now going to prepare a dietary sherbet éclair sundae for each guest after their steak dinner.

After a satisfied, muted grunting and groaning from the calorie-conscious group, the true surprise of the evening was forthcoming.

Tiffany stunned them all with a virtuoso hour-and-a-half concert on the Steinway grand as her bar boy chef offered each guest an "angel tip" after-dinner drink.

Beginning with the staid Beethoven *Moonlight Sonata*, she pleased them all to eye-glazing euphoria by switching to Debussey's *Clair de Lune*, and selected movements from Rachmaninoff's *First, Second, Third,* and *Fourth Piano Concertos*, all with many appoggiaturas as her personal enhancement.

Then, updating, she eased into Gershwin with selections from *An American in Paris, Porgy and Bess* with a concerto version of *Summertime and Bess* combined, finishing with Gershwin's classic *Rhapsody in Blue*, playing it even better than Gershwin had himself recorded it on Keystone Music Company player piano rolls.

"He played it too fast," Tiffany explained to her delighted audience.

As Pickle Club members were leaving, they all complimented their hostess on a wonderfully delicious and entertaining evening, with high praise for Tiffany's dinner table décor with Lincoln and Washington birthday decorator pieces combined with Valentine's Day imprinted napkins.

The group also departed Tiffany's grandly decorated and furnished West Des Moines condominium that crisp February night with a new appreciation and personal appraisal of her. All but one.

"How could such a lovely and talented girl, really, become a prostitute?" Rosemary *thought fiercely.*

CHAPTER V

DINNER AT MARGARET'S

After all the members of the Pickle Club had arrived at Margaret's palatial, two-story luxury condominium a few miles north but near Des Moines, adjacent to the fifth hole of the Briarcliff Golf Course in Ankeny, Marilyn, always the jokester, opened the conversation with a joke:

"'Mommy, Mommy, the kids at school are making fun of me. Am I really a werewolf?'"

"'Of course, not, dear. Hold still and let me comb your face again.'"

"Gaud, ain't that awful?" admitted Marilyn, after everyone had guffawed anyway.

"Tiffany, I didn't notice or hear your dog at our last dinner," asked Marilyn in a quick recovery.

"I had him in his big cage in my heated garage," explained Tiffany. "He's really good natured like most Labs, and he doesn't bark too often, but he is a good watchdog. If he hears a strange voice or sound, often he'll bark . . . ," she explained.

"Especially at loud noises. Last Fourth of July, he went crazy when the kids on our block lit their illegal fireworks their dads had gotten them from Missouri.

"It's instinctive, I guess. They relate the 'bang bangs' with shotguns and hunting . . ."

"Is he a retriever?" asked Mollie.

"I think all Labs are, naturally, but he's never been 'voice-command' trained for hunting. I've trained him to sit, roll over, shake hands, but that's about it . . . Do you know Labs have webbed feet? That's why they swim so well," Tiffany revealed.

"Well, being a short hair, he's probably easy to maintain, isn't he?" questioned Angie.

"Yes," responded Tiffany, "he is. But I don't really get into baths and tooth brushing and all that. I have experts do that for me. It doesn't cost that much."

"Tooth brushing for dogs?" a puzzled Margaret asked.

"And cats," answered Tiffany. "I have a Pet Mobile come out to the condo, usually Saturdays, once a month, for a 15-step wash and groom for Charlie, in a heated hydrobath. The say a dog's teeth should really be brushed twice a week . . ."

"Why? Plaque?" asked Margaret.

"That, and periodontal disease. You've seen old dogs with half their teeth gone. It's a disaster for them to eat."

"Can I come out, too? Sounds like a good opportunity for a hot tub," quipped Marilyn.

Meanwhile, as Margaret's Swedish live-in maid, Margot, served a tastefully sweet angelica wine to the group . . .

"Too many hangovers from those damn Devil's tails," said Margaret. "Great going down, but they do rattle around a bit. Sure froze response time the next day," she growled.

The group did unanimously notice the blossoming change in Tiffany over the five months they had known her. Although still very poised, she was losing her shyness and coming through as an alert, very intelligent and talented young woman.

Members of the Pickle Club were, whether they realized it or not, shifting their oversight and helpful hints attitudes from the youngest (and least mature) members of the group, Mollie and Angie, to Tiffany. Maternal instinct predominates in women, and this group let it flow freely now . . . towards Tiffany.

They all knew that self-esteem and self-satisfaction, using your personal gifts to achieve goals, are two of the most important attributes anyone can possess.

And they all knew that Tiffany had to develop these characteristics more. And they would help her. And she was responding remarkably well.

"And while we're talking about Charlie," Tiffany added, "I've got him insured with the Pet Partners, Inc., a North Carolina company that's affiliated with the American Kennel Club. I've got a small deductible to pay, but for about $800 a year premium, I've got their Essential Plus coverage policy, which covers preventive care and checkups every year. Of course, Charlie has already had his worm and other shots, nails clipped by the Pet Mobile people. And did you know, my agent tells me, only less than one percent of some 140 million pet dogs and cats in the United States are covered by insurance?"

"Didn't know there was any pet insurance available," said Rosie, stifling a yawn.

"I'm boring you. I'm sorry," Tiffany said. But plunging on, she added half defensively, "I'll bet you didn't know that half of the pets in Sweden are insured."

"Dinner's on!" announced Margaret. "Bring your glasses with you, 'cause we're having baked spice ham and duck. The ham was a favorite of Thomas Jefferson, the duck's courtesy of one of my boys' last hunting trip."

"Oh, I like your centerpiece," blathered Angie.

They all fixed their eyes on the lovely mix of roses and mums with baby breath and leaf add-ins gracing a beautiful white vase-urn with a white swan on either side, starkly contrasted against the red tablecloth. Members of the Pickle Club were all very attuned to the table décor and silver of their hostesses, appreciating and stealing ideas.

(They are still talking about the stellar table arrangement at Tiffany's with genuine white Havilland China and heavy sterling silver. And the gorgeous crystal goblets.)

At Margaret's dinner table they admired the Bavarian China, massive ornate sterling silver, Steuben glassware, and commented on her kitchen in bleached maple with white marble countertops.

"The wine you've been drinking is from Villary, Hungary. It's their best Villaenyer Auslesered Angelica . . ."

"And what about the ham?" asked Rosie, as they all were seated, de-ringing napkins and plunging into their salads. "How'd you do it?"

"Let me have Margot tell you," answered Margaret. A heavyset, but pretty, Margot, in full maid's apron uniform with white cap, appeared and said with a heavy Swedish accent, "This is a very special recipe, 17 pounds soaked overnight in cold water. Then simmered for three hours. Then cooled in that same water. Then trimmed.

"Into the baking pan," she continued, "with lots of cloves and brown sugar added. Then bake for two and a half hours, basted with red wine . . ."

"And the ducks?" prodded Margaret.

"Three-hour basting roast, again with red wine," answered Margot.

After the salads, Margot brought out the ham and ducks on huge silver platters, and the Pickle Club settled in for a long ordeal of feasting, contented smiles on their faces.

Margaret was a trained dinner crowd pleaser. Born in Corydon, in south-central Iowa, her father owned a small manufacturing company, subcontracting parts for the huge John Deere and McCormick farm machinery companies. Her mother pampered her at home but trained her in the basics, as all attentive mothers do.

But rather than take only her mother's word and practices for anything domestic, her parents sent Margaret to one of the finest finishing schools in the United States, the exclusive Stephens College in Columbia, Missouri. (That's how Margaret got into the Pickle Club—through Marilyn who was impressed with her when as president of the Stephens College Alumnae Club of Iowa, she personally invited her to join the Pickle Club.)

Marilyn saw her as a five-foot four, wren-like, mousy-haired "plain Jane," but not ugly or homely. Just plain, but friendly, sophisticated, and terribly smart. And it showed when she opened her thin-lipped mouth. Always well-dressed in the latest Nicole Miller and Versace fashions, she was a class act.

By the time Margaret graduated from Drake University in Des Moines with a major in business to get her CPA designation in accounting, she thought she knew how to run a company. But her father brought her into his company as a trainee and taught her the real world of manufacturing from the ground up.

"Keep a notebook and pencil in your hand," he ordered.

Then Margaret married her first husband, helping him with accounting and inventory for her small manufacturing company, making nozzles for jet engines.

As that company prospered with Margaret's expert guidance from home, she gradually withdrew to have her four boys, all born about two years apart. But after eight years, her husband's excessive drinking drove them apart, and the manufacturing business revenue declined. They divorced and Margaret got a handsome settlement. With this, she started another manufacturing company in Nevada, about thirty miles north and east of Des Moines.

Margaret began small, making popcorn machines, remarried, taking her second husband into the business as an accountant with her. And it grew quickly. They expanded into making cotton candy machines and hotdog and corndog machines with eventual worldwide distribution.

She became a millionaire many times over as her boys were now going through high school and entering college. Margaret's second husband, as their success grew, found he had time to date other women with Margaret working 60—and 70-hour weeks, getting her boys educated, and furthering her business interests.

Her sons finally persuaded her to divorce her second husband for adultery, forcing him to forego any interest in the business as a settlement.

Margaret then traveled the world, checking her company's distribution channels and representing Rotary International at various exhibitions, taking one or two of her sons with her at different times.

These were the two who now are vice presidents of her company, Pinnacle International, Inc., one as executive vice president, the other vice president of marketing. Margaret remains president and CEO of the firm.

Her other sons have done well: One is head of the Pharmaceutical Department at the University of Iowa; the other is head of Pediatrics at Iowa Methodist Medical Center in Des Moines, after graduating from the University of Iowa Medical School and interning at the Mayo Clinic in Rochester, Minnesota.

Meanwhile, Margaret's manufacturing concern had become so successful, she has just opened a new 300,000 square foot factory, partly on the same site as the old one.

And twice a week she takes the money rolling in to the bank in Nevada, in which she owns a large portion of stock.

Members of the Pickle Club had been to Margaret's home before, but they still visited and gossiped by phone for days afterwards about the luxury of her condominium in Ankeny: The full, wall-to-wall, floor-to-ceiling, walnut bookcases full of classics and bestsellers, the pecky Cyprus and walnut paneling, the lush white carpet contrasting red leather sofas and chairs with a smattering of black leather Windsor and gold French and Empire—Egyptian chairs and ottomans under colorful antique Venetian tapestries on two walls. Always causing comment was her trophy case showing off her citations from Rotary International with photos of Margaret shaking hands or just posing with presidents, governors, mayors, and other domestic and foreign dignitaries.

She prides herself on being a participant or contributor to a number of political campaigns.

And, of course, as the members of the Pickle Club strolled about Margaret's luxury condo, they again admired the art gracing the walls: An original Picasso, Degas, Cezanne, Utrillo, and a Winslow watercolor.

CHAPTER VI

DINNER AT MARILYN'S

Her husband calls her "Sunshine." Her many friends call her frequently on the phone and always hang up uplifted and/or enlightened. Or were happy to meet her for coffee or lunch. For Marilyn had that happy and instinctive insight into human nature and its many problems that made her a standout and interesting person.

A born entertainer with a remarkable sense of humor, she had won first place awards at Wapello, Iowa, High School in speech and drama and was presented the prestigious Iowa Girls Athletic Association first place award for her achievement as a high school cheerleader for three years.

All through her years in grade school and particularly high school, she exhibited a strong compassion and empathy for those less fortunate than she.

In the small town of Wapello, Marilyn's home was never far from either the grade school or high school. Her father was Louisa County Auditor, later mayor, and had offices in the courthouse near the schools.

So Marilyn would bring home with her for lunch, the poor kids or the farm kids who forgot their lunch, and then help her mother prepare a good noonday meal for them.

In grade school she would sympathize with girls who didn't have long socks like hers, so she would roll hers down or take them off to make them feel better.

Award-winning Marilyn was so lively, entertaining and sought after that the exclusive Stephens College in Columbia, Missouri, recruited her to enroll there.

And she did, majoring in business. (She really wanted to major in drama, but her practical politician-businessman-farmer father asked, "Can you get a job acting?")

So, after graduation and a couple secretarial positions with insurance companies in Des Moines, she moved up to office manager positions with a number of prestigious groups: The Iowa Employers Association, the Iowa Bankers Association, and the IGF Insurance Company, insuring Iowa feed and grain mills.

She and her public relations executive husband, Donald, then bought the two well-known Codners Florist and Greenery Stores with a mammoth plantscaping division, and expanded it to five stores in the Des Moines area.

As President of the entire operation, she enjoyed overseeing for six years some 40 employees and their plantscaping of some of Des Moines' largest offices and office buildings.

She has just retired after also serving as president of three TTT chapters, philanthropic charity groups sending dozens of underprivileged children to TTT Summer Camps in Eden Valley, Minnesota, each year; helping found the huge Blank Park Zoo in Des Moines, with the help of Des Moines Mayor Charles F. Iles and theater magnate Myron Blank, as the first president of the Iowa Zoological Society, and becoming President of the Stephens College Alumnae Club of Iowa.

Marilyn is a very charming, pretty blonde with a classic-sculpted symmetrical face with a wide, almost pouty mouth and generous lips, creamy complexion, wide eyebrows over blue-gray eyes and a petite, pretty nose.

She is well built, with a calm poise about her that marks her as someone anyone would want to know.

Extremely popular in high school and college, her true beauty jumped out at you when she flashed her big smile and purred a joke or one-liner at you with a husky, resilient voice.

Her one drawback: she didn't photograph well in action or even posed pictures. But in portraits she always appeared as a knockout.

Marilyn has a lusty laugh to match her hearty, earthy sense of humor. Even a slightly off-color joke comes from her with a clean sugarcoating.

It was her brilliant personality and being a good ballroom dancer that had won her many dates and lifelong friends, but it was not always evident. For she had her calmer moments of contemplation, usually spent thinking of ways she could help someone or make them happy. And this included to a large measure her husband Donald, who had dated enough to know when they married long ago that he'd found a real treasure.

Their two children, a boy and a girl, had grown up, gone through college, both graduating with master's degrees, had good jobs, and were now happily married.

Pickle Club members were always happy to get to go to Marilyn's house because they knew they'd get carefully selected aperitifs, good drinks, and a super dinner, always with some special entertainment. And this night was to be no exception to these expectations.

"Everybody want to try a Stone Fence?" Marilyn announced, rubbing her hands together.

All but one or two nodded in assent.

Angie, one of the two hesitants, said, "What the hell is that?"

"It's spiced scotch with apple cider cocktail," said Marilyn. "The cider sweetens the scotch for those who haven't had much of it."

"Sounds interesting. Let 'er rip," said Angie, rubbing her hands together, with Mollie then nodding.

Marilyn said honestly that she and her husband had been gifted with so much scotch for Christmas that she was happy to share it. "Besides, these are easy drinks to make . . .

"Help yourself to the special dip I made for you—clam chowder with mixed cream cheeses."

And, they did, glancing about Marilyn's well-decorated house, a handsome, five-level stone and frame structure on a large, sloping corner lot with seven rock gardens and twenty-two trees.

The couple bought it as the featured showplace of that year's Des Moines Home Show located in the exclusive Knolls section of West Des Moines.

Earth tones predominate throughout the house with suede leather and colonial maple in the family room with floor-to-ceiling and wall-to-wall bleached birch bookshelves housing classics and recent bestsellers. One entire brick wall houses a large fireplace with more birch bookshelves, heavy with leather-bound classics, reference books, and antique and modern ceramic pieces.

The lavishly decorated home features five fireplaces in all, with a more formal, traditionally decorated front room and dining area with walnut and mahogany furnishings in both. And both with fireplaces.

Sculptures throughout the house had been tastefully selected: a number of modern and classic Rodinesque figures, some moderns by Michael Aram; with oil paintings of scenes and flowers, colonial period portraits, and a genuine Renoir. The featured art hanging in the foyer of the house, a 4-foot by 5½-foot antique oil painting of three English greyhounds, matches the earth tones of the home ideally . . . Exquisite antiques are scattered here and there. Such as a hand-carved French settee that graces the foyer under the greyhound dog painting. It is valued at $5,000.

"Love your dip," said next-door neighbor Rosie to Marilyn. "I must get your recipe."

"I'll copy it and give it to you before you leave," answered Marilyn. "How'd you guys like the Stone Fences?" she questioned.

A few "umm's" and "very good's" were her answers.

"But it tastes a little like sweetened varnish," grouched Angie, rolling her eyes.

"Oh?" said Marilyn. "I've never drank any of that; but I'll get you something else."

"No, this is fine," replied Angie, a little embarrassed.

"Well, you heard about the guy who accidentally drank varnish, didn't you?" asked Marilyn, directing her comment to Angie directly.

"Well, nooo . . ."

"He died. It was an awful sight. But he sure had a beautiful finish . . . ," Marilyn quipped. Everyone laughed, Marilyn grinned.

"Anyhow, it's free," Rosie said, an edge on her voice as she leaned over to daughter Mollie.

The entire Pickle Club eagerly anticipated their March dinner meeting at Marilyn's, because they knew they would get (and had requested) Marilyn's specialty—baked baby-back pork ribs and sauerkraut.

Rosie often said this gal Marilyn could do wonders with brown sugar. It was in the kraut and the ribs dressing, as the six or eight pork racks cooked for four hours in a huge, covered steel boat-shaped baking pan. She also added apple slices to the kraut for a distinct flavoring.

Marilyn's other specialty, she sometimes served the Pickle Club, was spaghetti and meatballs, again with brown sugar neutralizing the spicing of the meat and giving it a distinct flavor.

"Ah, yes," she said. "It isn't just using brown sugar in cooking. It's knowing *how much* to put in any given recipe."

"Oh, I just love your spring floral centerpiece," exclaimed Tiffany as the group began salads at the big table in Marilyn's spacious dining room.

"What are those?" she asked with a quizzical frown.

"Red, yellow and pink gerbera daisies with baby breath, caspia and two kinds of gypsophila dressings," Marilyn explained.

"It is lovely," Tiffany responded, accompanied by assenting nods from around the table as they turned to banter and small talk in pairs.

"You're all done selling your flower shops and plantscaping operations, Marilyn?" questioned Rosie.

"Yep. It was fun while it lasted. But a lot of work. Which I thoroughly enjoyed. But there comes a time to call a halt to a slim-skinned profit margin operation and its headaches.

"The supermarket chains, one in particular, really cut into our volume, and they could do it easily . . ."

Marilyn paused and rose to help Katie and Rosie gather up the salad plates and serve the ribs and kraut with green beans and French bread.

"How's that?" queried Margaret, always on the lookout for business information.

"Well, in your business, Margaret," Marilyn answered, turning, "your margins are probably based on labor and other standing overhead costs—acquisition of raw materials, die changes and replacements and so forth.

"In the florist business, we have to look at not only standing overhead, particularly like rents and wholesale costs, which figure in our COGS (cost of goods sold), but dumpage—the amount of spoiled flowers, plants and ferns we have to throw away almost daily.

"The big supermarkets had us for lunch every day," Marilyn continued as she sat down, "because they could own their own wholesale houses, grow their own flowers and plants, and they had no rents to pay, since most of them had their shops in their stores. That's where it's all at in the florist business—owning your own real estate. Look at McDonald's. They own all their sites.

"We were paying $6,000 a month rent in one location downtown, escalating wholesale costs. And increasing gas prices really cost us a lot of money for our five delivery vans.

"We were doing $3 million gross a year, but with only a 2½% profit margin . . . that's about what banks make."

"Gaud. That's awful," Margaret exclaimed.

"Yeah. But it was a lot of fun. I enjoyed working with our hundreds of good customers. But there comes a time . . ."

"Yeah. Right," Margaret agreed.

"Your ribs and everything are just delicious," Tiffany observed. "I've got to learn more about cooking," she said matter-of-factly.

"Thank you all," said Marilyn, in response to the generous sweep of accolades around the table.

"Save some room for the strawberry shortcake comin' up," she added.

After dessert, they adjourned to the downstairs two-level knotty-pine game room to shoot pool, watch the fire in the stone fireplace and gossip, and again comment on the maintenance it must take for the patterned parquet wood floors on the fourth level above, in the foyer and in the huge kitchen.

The group also many times commented individually on Marilyn's brilliant use of colors in her home and in those she selected in her always best-dressed designer fashions of Flora Kunz, Louis Marino, Renlyn of New York, William Royce, and Valentino, that she wore.

The game room now had been Marilyn's son's room when he came home from college. It sported full, wall-to-wall birch bookcases, and a high-backed pine waterbed in one corner alongside a big armoire.

Marilyn brought brandy down eventually, totally and happily destroying the calorie count that week for almost everyone.

As they each stepped out into the brisk March night air to go home, they thought of all the things they could have brought up to question or discuss.

Was Tiffany looking for a man? That comment about cooking . . . Next time, perhaps.

CHAPTER VII

DINNER AT MOLLIE'S

Mollie and Angie live close to one another on Des Moines' west side, not far from Drake University. So, in similar economic circumstances, it was natural that they share Pickle Club hostessing. Both were very attractive 21-year-old girls who shared the same philosophy about many things: rock bands, boas, sequins, angora, high heels, Armani, Valentino, jeans, white and blue low-cut blouses, tattoos, and boys.

Mollie, who had just graduated as a landscape architect and, with her new husband, bought an older, newly remodeled house. Angie, who had been a waitress and bank clerk while attending Des Moines Area Community College and AIB, a Des Moines business college, had just landed a job with a large Des Moines based insurance company as a claims clerk and moved into a new, furnished apartment near Mollie. The company's human resource people promised to bring her along within the company, depending on her performance. So she planned to buy a house or condo soon.

Both were proud of the tattoos on their lower, well-contoured backsides.

"Why there?" chimed one of Angie's boyfriends and Mollie's husband. "Can't see it . . ."

Wellll . . . members of the Pickle Club didn't really look forward with great anticipation to their being entertained here, because they had already been through the drill: Franzia 12%, Chianti or Zinfandel wine from a five-liter plastic bag in a box, and potato chips with plain chive dip from a carton. Dinner could be a packaged macaroni and cheese dinner, or cooked, sliced ham, or Chinese. Or even pizza with a slaw salad.

"Give them a chance," defended Marilyn. "They're learning. Like most kids, they'll learn by watching and listening to us and doing things on their own.

"Besides, they don't have the money to work with that the rest of us do.

"And, really, it's the friendship, camaraderie, chatter, and gossip we all come for anyway."

"Well, I thought I taught her well as she was growing up," Rosie said. "At least how to cook and clean a little."

"Give her time, she'll get there," surmised Marilyn.

Sure enough, tonight's fare was Franzia's Chianti with a delivered, boxed pizza with Italian bread, packaged coleslaw, and a box cake.

Mollie's house was clean and simply furnished with an odd mix of early Sears-Roebuck furniture she and her husband had accumulated from garage sales and want ads. Some of it was new—the stove, refrigerator, microwave, and TV—but most of the remainder was plain mahogany with flowered cotton or tapestry fabric coverings and somewhat worn around the edges.

After a short while of chatter and banter, the quick buzz of the Chianti 12% wine set in, and Angie blurted out, "Tiffany, are you looking for a man?"

"Why, uh, why do you ask?" a startled Tiffany replied.

"I just thought maybe after your comment at our last dinner when you said you would have to learn more about cooking . . ."

"Oh, Lord, no. I was just thinking out loud. That's only one of a lot of things I have yet to learn."

"But you're so beautiful and talented." Marilyn interjected. "You could be a movie star . . . and certainly should have no trouble getting any guy that you settle on."

"You could certainly marry well," added Angie.

Tiffany hung her head, her expression saddening, "I'm so far behind," she said plaintively. "I just don't have any immediate plans, I guess. I don't know which way to go in any direction."

Marilyn, never one to mince words, straightened and threw her shoulders back. Looking first at Angie, then Mollie, she paused and phrased her words carefully. *"No one should use the past as an excuse for not moving ahead."*

Marilyn paused again, then continued, *"You can't be a quitter. Nothing is impossible if you believe in yourself. Everyone makes mistakes.*

"Learn from them, then move on."

Margaret leaned forward, looking at all three young girls. "Always do your best. And when that isn't good enough, *know in your mind that you did your best.* That's all you can do.

Margaret sat back. "Yes," she thought, "I could take Tiffany and send her to law school or at least to charm school, and then marry her off to my one single son left who's my vice president for marketing at the company.

"But, my God, she was a prostitute!"

"I agree with Margaret one hundred percent," said Marilyn. "All of us need to develop self-esteem and get satisfaction from using our natural gifts and aptitudes," continued Marilyn, smiling at Tiffany.

"And, if you don't agree, I'll take away all your crayons and coloring books . . . ," she cracked. "Maybe your jacks, too."

That bit of philosophy highlighted her own secret only Marilyn and her husband knew: for all her accomplishments and social poise, Marilyn herself had overcome a serious inferiority complex that began for her at puberty.

She knew it sprang from her overly practical father who often, although loving her dearly, treated her as a smart aleck and told her numerous times she "had a lot to learn." Like telling her she couldn't get a job acting after college even if she majored in drama.

Accompanying her husband Donald, continuously entertaining, many times, always dressed in handsome clothes or goddess party dresses, influential politicians, stage, screen, and sports celebrities, and traveling with him throughout the United States to do so, she worked at her craft to charm and became better at it than the influential people they were entertaining. Better than anybody, if she really turned it on. So she knew what it takes . . .

After all, she was Wapello's sweetheart from her toddler days, and people still talk about what a "darlin' child she was with those long, blonde curls and all . . ."

"We all need to continue to strive all the time. Love it. Cherish it. Be thankful for your gifts and be persistent. And generous in your giving to others," overachiever Marilyn concluded.

"You know," Margaret continued, "Marilyn's exactly right; self-esteem is one of the most important attributes anyone can have. As a matter of fact, while I was in London recently, teachers there told me they are banning the word 'failure' from their classrooms, and replacing that word with 'deferred success.' Just to boost the morale of marginal students . . ."

"Yo," interrupted Mollie. "This is just like being in church."

"Yeah, and you need it," snapped her mother Rosie. "Pay attention. You just got a good lecture from two of the most successful women in our Pickle Club. And it was free."

Not being experienced enough yet to keep a conversation going as hostess, the table talk lagged slightly during the pizza dinner the girls hurriedly served.

Marilyn picked it up for them as they began finishing their pizzas:

"Hey, guys. Bought anything interesting lately from your favorite clothes shops?" she asked.

Mollie had bought a new leather jacket at a spring sale; Angie had picked up a silk kimono and scoop-neck maillot with a matching swim skirt for the coming season that she was excited about.

"I think I'm a compulsive shopper," Angie confessed. "I just love to prowl the stores . . ."

"I don't think you are," retorted Mollie. "You don't buy everything you look at. Now, that's a compulsive shopper."

"Oh?"

"Yes. I've heard of a family where the mother bought six packages of clothespins and didn't even have a clothesline. That's a compulsive shopper," said Mollie.

"Maybe she was going to put one up," interjected Marilyn.

"No. She just likes to buy clothespins," smiled Mollie.

"You know, compulsive shopping is being looked at much like compulsive gambling or drinking or using drugs," Marilyn observed. "It's not a silly or a selective habit. It's a mental disorder."

"How the hell do you treat compulsive shoppers?" mocked Angie.

"Well, I think doctors have been prescribing the antidepressant Celexa for starters. I don't know much more about it than that," Marilyn said.

"Jeez. It takes all kinds . . . ," muttered Angie. "But I do have a thing about halter tops . . ."

"I'm having trouble with my kid," Katie burst out.

"Oh, how's that?" questioned Leyria who seldom got into general discussions but was rather content to listen and observe. "How old is he?"

"Fourteen."

"What's the problem?" Leyria asked.

"Well, he's down in his studies. Won't do homework. Won't get a part-time job. Won't do a lot of things we ask him to."

"Sounds like a typical teenage hormone rebellion," mused Leyria. "My husband, the judge, doesn't handle any juvenile cases now, but he did as a lawyer. He'd say, 'threaten 'em with military school. And follow through with it if nothing else works.' It's not all that bad. It really is a pretty good idea. That was the problem Donald Trump's parents had with him. And look how he turned out . . ."

"Yeah, but his folks were also millionaires," chortled Margaret.

"Seriously, pay more attention to him."

"We do," Katie said plaintively. "We do. My husband spoils him with gifts, got him a driver's permit. He wrecked the car. Got him a part-time job and he insulted the customers."

Katie's boy, a son by her first husband, a Korean college professor, was a dark, curly-haired, typical Korean.

"Maybe he feels he doesn't fit in," Leyria continued. "Get him into group activity like the Boy Scouts or Sea Scouts. Then pay personal attention to him. Have your husband play catch, baseball, or football with him. Get him into little league baseball, soccer, or hockey."

Marilyn chimed in, "Go with him to the practices and the games. Spend time with him. Does he have any close friends?"

"No," Katie answered. "And he's not athletic."

"Then get him a tuba or into piano lessons," Tiffany suggested hesitantly.

"Okay. Sounds good. You've given me some ideas. We'll give them a try."

"Well, if he gets into any group activity at all, hopefully he'll hook up with some new guy friends," Marilyn added hopefully.

"And tell your husband you'll do the housework now and cut back on your golf games," Marilyn added, her voice slightly rising with an edge, to make the point.

"Have to," said Katie, smiling gingerly.

CHAPTER VIII

DINNER AT ROSEMARY'S

Rosemary's condominium is just a few blocks from the big houses of Marilyn, Rosie, and Katie. It is one of 22 in a group and is simply furnished in a mix of comfortable colonial maple and contemporary. The colors are well defined, light browns and greens, with a large yellow, tiled kitchen, lavender bathrooms, and teal carpeting throughout.

Rosemary has done all the decorating and remodeling, as she has for numerous people and their houses, apartments, and townhouses.

For this is what she has been doing for almost 20 years since her husband walked out on her and left her high, dry, and penniless, with a houseful of five kids. "Never did know where he went," she told the Pickle Club members. "But I knew in short order he was gone for good."

Rosemary is a large-framed woman, attractive, with a mercurial temperament, very strong; and a workhorse when she gets started on a job.

She knew she had to do something right away, so she refinanced her house, took the money to buy other houses, good-looking on the outside but needing internal fixing up. She subbed out the electrical and plumbing work. And made a go of remodeling and selling the houses for a profit.

A healthy German farm-girl, raised with the fear of God, justice for all, and a strong work ethic, her skills improved as did the quality of her jobs. She had her kids who could, help her along the way, and soon she began to realize a good profit for her hard work.

She sold her own house when the last child left home to marry, and bought her present condominium, paying cash, and began studying and cautiously playing the investments markets. She is now beginning to see some substantial gains in her investments.

Tonight she is serving soup and crumpets, she calls them, beef stew, one of her specialties, with all the ingredients put together carefully item by item, like the beef, and served with crumpet-size grilled cheese and beef-sliced snack sandwiches. A blue-cheese salad dressing covers the generous salads, and she serves a cold, light lager beer with the dinner, followed by espresso coffee in demitasse cups with freshly baked cherry and French apple pies.

Seating is a bit cramped around the table, even with an extra leaf in the table and expanded with three folding chairs.

"I have a surprise for you all tonight. I've been dying to tell you. But I wanted to wait until it opened here. I've been taking my other friends to see it this week at the West Des Moines Sierra Theater," Rosemary announced.

"I've a small part in the movie, 'Her Majesty.'"

"My gosh, tell us about *that*!" Norma exclaimed.

"Well, I'll not only going to tell you about it, show you some pictures we took there on the set, but then we'll all take two cars and go see it. On me. How's that?"

A murmur of gratitude and anticipation swept around the table.

"You remember the round-the-world trip my sister Karen and I took three years ago?" Rosemary began.

Nods again around the table.

"Well, our last stop was in Cambridge, New Zealand, where the movie 'Her Majesty' was being shot. My sister, who lives in San Francisco, knows the parents of the film's director, Mark J. Gordon. Well, this connection got us both parts in the movie, which they were just doing the last casting of.

"Here are some pictures we took on the sets," said Rosemary, handing out two small sets of photographs.

"I've been having a lot of fun seeing the movie with my golfing buddies and other friends, and I couldn't wait to tell you guys about it.

"I took some pictures, and my sister took some. When we were in scenes together, we had the photographs taken by onlookers or other cast members who weren't being photographed. You can see me waving a British flag from a balcony and walking in a parade during the last few scenes of the movie. I'm wearing a hat and white dress with purple and teal flowers.

"You can see Karen and me in two of the still pictures you're looking at. We took part in two scenes. Each was shot twice before the director was satisfied."

"Yes, I can see you guys here," exclaimed Marilyn, pointing them out to the others as she passed the photographs along.

"The whole operation of producing a movie is a big deal," Rosemary pointed out. "It's amazing how much manpower it takes to film even just one little scene."

She explained that there were at least a thousand extras brought into the town to film the parade scenes.

"What's the story of the picture?" asked Rosie.

"I was really pleased with the family nature of this movie," Rosemary answered. "It's set in 1953 when a young girl learns that her idol, Queen Elizabeth, will be visiting Middleton, where she lives," Rosemary began.

"Along with her other adventures, she meets a poor, old woman whose home is in danger of being destroyed to make way for the big parades of Queen Elizabeth and entourage during her visit.

"I don't want to give away the plot of the movie. I'll let you see how it works out. But the film has a great many family messages with good, wholesome fun here and there . . ."

"Hasn't it just been released here in this country?" asked Angie.

"It's an independent picture first released in other countries before getting here now," Rosemary explained.

"Our show starts at nine, so we've got about an hour to get there. We should probably leave in about forty minutes."

"Good," said Katie. "Let's clean up the dishes, pack up the lucky husband's pie, and leave in about forty minutes. All right?"

"Okay," said Rosemary. "The theater has roped off a section of seating for us, so we can go right in . . ."

"You know," Marilyn began, "we're really lucky to have these first-class theaters here in West Des Moines."

Nodding to the consensus, Marilyn continued, "In fact, the whole area of Des Moines has come a long way in the last 25 years."

"Be specific," Margaret prodded.

"I can remember when Des Moines had two bookstores, one for new books in Younkers Department Store balcony, the other a used bookstore in the old WHO Radio station building. And West Des Moines had two motorcycle cops for a police force.

"No art galleries, no art stores anywhere, and just two major department stores," Marilyn continued.

"The redevelopment began for Iowa in the sixties with legislation approving liquor by the drink, followed shortly by pari-mutuel horse betting at the new Prairie Meadows Racetrack and Casino."

"Who got all that started?" asked Mollie.

"Well, Governor Harold Hughes first said we ought to legalize liquor by the drink so we can control it," Marilyn explained.

Hubby Don knew the old Iowa State Fair Secretary Ken Fulk who was trying to get pari-mutuel horse betting legalized for the State Fair.

"People generally thought it was the gamblers who wanted it. Not at all. It was the horse breeders," Marilyn continued.

"Finally got that, along with a new racetrack and casino, which now has table games as well as slot machines. Just like Las Vegas. Everything except Keno, roulette and sports betting. Now we've got nine gambling casinos around the state of Iowa and more being constructed in private resort areas like Spirit Lake.

"Along the way, the Iowa Lottery got going, headquartered here in West Des Moines, by the way. Now it's operated in over twenty states. No one from Iowa ever wins it, but it brings in a lot of money for the state. People are finding out that agriculture, insurance and small manufacturing can't adequately fuel this state's economy.

"So now it's gambling, horseracing, farms, insurance and small manufacturing that fuel Iowa's economy. Right?" Margaret said. "Don't forget, I'm one of the larger manufacturers."

"Not for a minute," said Marilyn.

"But now with gambling, expanding insurance operations, new biodiesel and ethanol plants throughout the state, we got 'er going good," said Margaret.

"Right. We've seen downtown literally explode with the new Principal Baseball Stadium, Grand Avenue and Locust Street Parkway, the new Des Moines Library, the new Des Moines Science Center, Poppajohn Education Center, and the new Meredith Publishing Park around their big office buildings. And don't forget the expanded Des Moines Art Center, new Convention Center, and the huge, just-opened Wells Fargo Events Center with Paul McCartney as one of the opening events.

"And," Marilyn continued, "now we've got five private, art-for-sale art galleries in Des Moines, three riverboats for gambling along with other casinos throughout Iowa, and the lottery (which is just the old numbers game) fueling a complete rebuilding of our Des Moines area economy. And with mostly all newly remodeled streets and interstates, inter-city highways, along with most of our schools rebuilt.

"And don't forget five developers building condos and apartment buildings now out of a half dozen old, downtown Des Moines office buildings," Margaret added.

"And presently," Marilyn interjected, "we've got more and better movie theaters, a performing arts theater—the Stoner Theater, Civic Center, Temple for the Performing Arts, and more in four major, huge shopping malls with a total of ten theaters. And a fifth shopping mall is under construction . . ."

"Gaud almighty!" Angie exclaimed. "You guys sound like a couple chambers of commerce.

"Well," said Marilyn, "I think we're all pretty proud of how far we've come in a relatively short time."

"Yeah, but," added Rosie, "half the small towns in this state are boarded up, though—"

"Well, it seems so. But many have a lot of boarded windows in their business sections, and this makes the largest cities in the state centers of attraction for business and entertainment," declared Marilyn. "I know my hometown of Wapello seems to be half boarded up. But that's the price of progress. Business in the state is becoming more centralized in the urban areas, and that's why they're being made so attractive."

"You guys ready to go see a good show?" said Rosemary.

"Yeah," said Rosie. "We can take my car."

"And mine," said Rosemary. "We can all get in the two of them, I think. It's a beautiful spring evening, so it'll be fun to get out."

CHAPTER IX

DINNER AT KATIE'S

"Really had a great time watching you and your sister Karen in 'Her Majesty,'" commented Marilyn to Rosemary, as the Pickle Club gathered at Katie's for their June dinner.

"Had a little trouble spotting Karen myself at first," said Rosemary. "She wasn't right out there in front like me, but you kinda have to look close to find us in the second scene.

"I'm no trouble to find in the balcony shot of the parade scene, since I'm waving a British flag. But after that it's oblivion, I'm afraid. But it was fun, and we both earned extra pay for two days. And met a lot of interesting people. I've never been on a movie set before . . ."

Katie's large, tri-level home is across the street and a little down the block from Marilyn's big house on the corner and Rosie's home in back of Marilyn's on the next street. It is nicely furnished in modern chair/sofas, occasional chair/ottoman sets in rusts with deep red and white contrasting walls setting them off. The dining room is papered with Korean garden scenes of predominant rusts and lovely Korean garden and gentle water scenes with many flowers to adorn the wall. White statuary, modern sculptures, and Asian candle lanterns grace the corners of the living and dining rooms. An Asian floor screen partially separates the two rooms.

Katie is a Korean beauty. Tall, slender, athletic, she speaks English very well but with a slight accent. She is an expert at Korean culinary art, and the Des Moines Golf and County Club ladies golf champion for three years in a row.

"But that's it," says her loving insurance company president husband, laughing. I do most all the housework and a lot of the cooking. Because Katie practices golf shots and plays a lot during the spring and summer.

"You guys are lucky to get her cooking tonight this early in the golf season," smiles her husband Cliff to the group, dashing out the door for his monthly poker club session with buddies.

Katie's only diversion from her husband, son, and golf is her small garden just off the spacious patio in back of her house.

Here plants of Korean map leaves, three-tiered pagodas and Shanghai candle lanterns on stands grace the walk around a lacy Korean maple tree growing out of red lava rocks.

Katie has carefully planted prairie, savanna, and woodland plants here and there "to get a mix of Oriental with native Iowa," according to Katie in describing it.

Marilyn designed the plantings for her and recommended the mix. Husband Cliff cheerfully paid for the whole thing. Eyeing the finished garden in early April, he snorted, "I hope this gives her some earthy experience. And a touch of puttering."

"Sure has," said Marilyn and Katie, gleefully planning additional black-eyed Susans, butterfly milkweed and cinnamon-scented milkweed, prairie sky switch grass, dropseed grass, nodding alliums, and lead plants with a Culver root here and there.

"Damn, this *is* fun," Katie happily exclaimed.

"Now, if the critters will leave this stuff alone . . . ," said Marilyn philosophically.

Katie grew up on a small farm outside Seoul, capital of South Korea, shortly after hostilities ceased and the war-torn and drained country struggled to regain its equilibrium.

Though her family were all fairly well educated—her father and uncle were engineers who farmed for family food and worked in a nearby Seoul factory—their farm home still had dirt floors, a well, and outdoor privies.

Katie had ambitions. She studied hard, learned English, and as a very pretty teenager, married a young college professor at the university in Seoul where she was a freshman.

They moved to America shortly after the birth of her son she is now having some problems with and has said her marriage was not working out either.

They separated, then divorced, after Katie met her present husband Cliff, moved in with him and married. Cliff is a devoted father to Katie's troubled boy but can't seem to get the combination to settle him down. His own two sons by a previous marriage are successful—one a lawyer, the other a doctor. But he's still trying.

"Katie, we all enjoy coming to your house for dinner, 'cause the Korean cuisine you cook for us is always good," quipped Marilyn, sitting down to enjoy her third toddy, a spiked rum and Coke from Katie's open bar in the kitchen.

"A toast." Marilyn proclaimed. "Here's to those I love; here's to those who love me; here's to those who love those I love; and here's to those who love those who love me. Cheers!"

"Right," observed Angie. "Are you ever serious, Marilyn?"

"Yes, I am," Marilyn declared, a mischievous glint in her eyes. "I have a sonnet for you all tonight, too," she announced to the group, now all attentive and relaxed, seated around Katie's large front room.

Katie stepped down from the kitchen to stand in the entryway where they were all sitting, as Marilyn began soberly:

> *Sometimes . . .*
> *When you cry . . .*
> *No one sees your tears . . .*
> *Sometimes . . .*
> *When you are in pain . . .*
> *No one sees your hurt . . .*
> *Sometimes . . .*
> *When you're worried . . .*
> *No one sees your stress . . .*

Marilyn glanced around the room, making sure everyone was sitting up straight in rapt attention. Frowns in some faces, pensive hurt on others, a grim smile on some, as she continued:

> *Sometimes . . .*
> *When you are happy . . .*
> *No one sees your smile . . .*
> *Or your tears of joy . . .*

And Marilyn paused for effect.

> *But fart just one time . . .*

"Oh, God, Marilyn. You're terrible," groused Katie.

"But fun," observed Margaret.

"You're sick," chortled Mollie.

"Who's sick?" retorted Marilyn:

> *"Mrs. Brown, can Sheldon come out and play?"*
> *"Now you children know he has leprosy."*
> *"Then can we come in and watch him rot?*

"Now . . . that's sick," Marilyn concluded.

"Oh, my God," drawled Katie, beating a hasty retreat back to the kitchen.

As they all began to sit down around Katie's enormous dining room table, Rosie mumbled, "Thanks for the floor show, Marilyn."

"Happy to oblige," Marilyn responded, adding, "Katie, your Asian lily centerpiece is just beautiful."

Everyone stared at the colorful arrangement in the center of the table in a large, flat, white bowl, contrasting the black tablecloth, heavy sterling silverware, and Chinese-Oriental napkin rings. Katie served fantail shrimp cocktails with Korean sauce, then Korean eggrolls on their salad plates with soy sauce. Several of the group commented that they tasted just like Chinese eggrolls. "Except a little different mix of vegetables," Katie pointed out, serving the main dishes of Rhee Beef and cashew chicken with Korean Tao dressing on the side.

"Hot damn, this is good," declared Angie.

"Yeah. Ya can't buy this stuff . . . ," Mollie observed soberly.

"Wait 'til you see dessert," declared Katie from the kitchen. "Got Emperor Bao sauce on vanilla ice cream, with Korean fortune cookies. And that's good. Forget your diets, kids." (pronouncing it "keeds") "Enjoy," Katie directed, bringing out a heavy tray of her Emperor Bao-sauced ice cream.

"Who the hell is Emperor Bao?" questioned Angie.

"A long lost Korean royalty?" suggested Norma, who seldom spoke up about anything.

"Or Japanese," chided Rosie, who knew Katie hated everything Japanese.

"Certainly not those people," Katie declared emphatically, sitting down.

"Why do you hate them so?" asked Rosie innocently.

"I've heard you berate them a number of times, and I've always wondered. They're our friends now, you know," said Marilyn.

"Oh, really?" Katie responded. Let me tell you a little story:

"Teddy Roosevelt handed Korea to the Japanese after negotiating the end to the Russian-Japanese War in 1905. He wanted to keep the Russians out of Korea and China. So he gave Korea to the Japs and won the Nobel Peace Prize for it.

"And of all the goddamn ironies," Katie continued, "he donated the thirty or forty thousand dollars he got from the Nobel Foundation to establish a Permanent Peace Committee.

"And another piece of shit about the Japs," Katie spat out, "do you know the Russian negotiators for the Russo-Japanese Peace Treaty were both Harvard grads, as was Teddy Roosevelt, who held two degrees from Harvard College . . ."

"Is that a reason to hate them?" asked Marilyn.

"No. Let me tell you what really happened then," Katie snapped. "This negotiation and treaty turned those Jap bozos loose on my country since they now virtually owned it.

"And they looted, raped, and killed without hesitation, provocation, or retribution. And they raped and killed my grandmother and her sister. In this horrible aftermath of Teddy Roosevelt's meddling. So there. That's why I hate 'em. Can't you see why?

"They still piss me up," she decreed, throwing her hands up in the air.

The Pickle Club members sat in stunned silence. They had never before seen the happy-go-lucky, always smiling Katie turn on a subject like this before. She was breathing heavily. Enraged, nostrils flared, like a wild animal cornered by a predator.

The salicitous Marilyn, trying to restore calm, stammered, "Tennis, anyone?"

CHAPTER X

PICNIC DINNER AT NORMA'S

"Feel better?" Marilyn asked Katie, nodding. Everyone was comfortably seated in large lawn chairs, colorful camp and folding chairs on Norma's triangular, shaded patio. A flowered trellis shaded the group from the sun as they sipped their Mai Tais and margaritas.

"What?" said Katie, a puzzled look spreading over her face.

"Your tirade on the Japanese of 1905," Marilyn answered.

"Oh, that. I think I said it all in my outburst at the last Pickle Club dinner—as you know.

"But on a positive note, I should say that at least women are making progress in Korea."

"How's that?" Marilyn asked.

"Well, you know, most Korean women have walked behind their husbands for centuries. Now they walk in front. Is this progress?"

"Sure seems to be," Marilyn answered enthusiastically.

"Well," Katie observed wryly, "there still are a lot of landmines left buried from the war there. Now, they all walk in front of their husbands."

Quietly changing the subject, Katie queried, "Is that a real diamond or a cubic zucchini?" pointing to Marilyn's large, marquis-cut diamond on her right hand.

"It's real," Marilyn answered, smiling at Katie's malapropism, one of many she still spoke. "You mean zircon . . ."

"Of course," said Katie, not a bit embarrassed.

Norma's home is a large, typical West Des Moines suburban style ranch, generously furnished with department store furniture and specialty store décor and knickknacks. The furnishings are well chosen, modern, but not expensive, in brown tapestry fabric with flowered, cotton-covered chairs.

Her bedrooms are cozy and chintzy, the tile bathrooms red and green with a carefully chosen assortment of decorator towels.

Norma is a quiet and intelligent person, not given to idle conversation, but she can keep up as long as you stay serious. Humor is beyond her. That's why she so admires Marilyn. Because as a human resources specialist, she knows that humor and personality combined are charming assets hard to come by.

Norma is a nice-looking, but plain, professional lady in her mid-forties. She always dresses well, with her makeup always very subdued.

"Where's Angie?" Norma asked. "She's the only one who's not here . . ."

"She's got a date," responds Mollie. "She called to tell me to tell you all she's sorry she couldn't break it. She doesn't get that many offers . . ."

"But she's so attractive," said Marilyn.

"And can dress up when she really wants to," said Katie.

"And she does," said Mollie, "even at work. But she doesn't suck up to guys like a lot of girls do to get dates."

"Maybe it's her makeup," observed Marilyn.

"Yeah, I think so," agreed Margaret.

"She does go a bit heavy on eye shadow," said Norma, who rarely made comments about anything, especially anything as arcane as women's makeup.

"Someone should tell her about the eye shadow. And the 'too-much' mascara," added Norma.

"What do you use, Marilyn?" asked Mollie. "You always look so pretty."

"Just Revlon base cream and a little brush-on powder. Very little, if any, eye stuff."

"You don't need much else," observed Katie.

"God, I do," said Mollie. I use Sheercover brush-on. Supposed to have minerals in it for bright skin color . . ."

"Does have," observed Leyria. "Do you know some ladies' shops and stylists have tattoo artists on staff to ink in eyebrows, eyeliner, even lipstick and skin-tone blot-outs of facial or body blotches?"

"Hey, that's got to look artificial," said Rosemary.

"It does," answered Leyria. "But it depends on the individual."

"Well, I have had bags under my eyes for years that me and Katie could carry our golf clubs in. You know what takes them down when they get big?"

The group, all alert to this discussion, almost in unison, voiced aloud, "What?!"

"Preparation H, the hemorrhoid ointment. Works for me."

"Know what dermatologists recommend?" asked Julie. "And I use the stuff."

Again, a loud, "What?" from the group.

"Kinerase. I use the skin cream and lotion. They're supposed to stop skin moisture loss."

"And doesn't it clog the skin pores?" asked Jackie.

"Right," declared Julie. "Also improves on wrinkles, sun damage to the skin, and especially freckles. Kinerase also has skin cleansers with green and white tea extracts and aloe vera that smooth out my skin," Julie continued.

"The stuff sure works for me," she concluded.

"I have dry skin sometimes," said Tiffany.

"You're so beautiful, you shouldn't need anything," declared Marilyn.

"Oh, but I do. I'm into Neostrata. It's available only through your doctor, but it really works for me. They say it's hyperkeratosis I have."

"But Neostrata also has good stuff for acne and oily skin. It all works . . . ," said Tiffany quietly.

"And then there's Botox for us old ladies who want to stay looking young," breathed Margaret.

"That's an injection, isn't it?" asked Mollie, making mental notes for the future.

"Yes. With a tiny needle administered only by a physician or registered nurse."

"Doesn't that go directly into the muscle under the wrinkles?" queried Katie.

"Yep. And some people get side effects like a headache, nausea, flu syndrome, or even temporary eye droop. But it works . . ."

"Yeah, but works for only about six months," quietly observed Rosie. "I tried it and gave it up. It's too expensive. I had my frown lines done. It really worked for a while. Movie stars, male and female, have it done all the time. Like every six months," said Rosie. "No anesthesia required, but I had an anesthetic cream application first. The whole procedure only takes about ten minutes."

"Well, back to Angie—many times you have to play up to guys, good makeup or not," chortled Rosie. "What about you, Tiffany? I bet you get hit on a lot. How 'bout that?"

"Not as often as you think," replied Tiffany. "Most guys coming to the library are married and/or bring their kids. The others who come in to reference their grade and high school work are too young."

"In between," she sighed, "there just aren't that many . . . Oh, I get asked out every once in a while, but I know those guys who ask me are just hot to trot—or are married. Or most of the ones who haven't wedding rings on don't really look like good prospects to me. I had a number of dates in college and in my younger teen years. But none seemed to get very serious."

"Maybe you're too particular," said Katie.

"I suppose so," Tiffany responded. "But I hate to waste an evening with someone who I know is a loser. Or going to be."

"Well, all I know is I've been very lucky," said Marilyn, smiling.

"Me, too," said several others.

Norma brought out a tray of drinks.

"What's the key to a successful marriage, Marilyn?" asked Katie, her own failed first marriage in mind.

"Make a good choice to start with. A lot of girls are too young when they marry. Or are too young to know what to look for if they're husband shopping," Marilyn replied.

"Like what?" asked Norma, whose marriage, now that her three children were grown up and had moved away, was teetering. She suspected her husband of infidelities.

"Well, you've got to trust one another. Be open and frank. No secrets. Be honest with one another. Have a mutual faith and respect for each other.

"And have fun," Marilyn continued. "That doesn't mean a rip-roaring ball all the time you're together. But dwell on your mutual interests and develop them. Make him laugh, even if his lips are chapped," Marilyn quipped.

"And a few other very important things. A woman has to make her husband feel irreplaceable. Play up to his ego. His abilities. Whatever he does, tell him he's remarkable and he's the best, whether it's at his job, making love, paying you simple courtesies, or whatever. It doesn't matter if you stretch the truth a little sometimes. He'll be pleased. But generally, you can do this sincerely.

"*Tell him frequently that you think the world of him and his capabilities. The whole world cycle of humanity survives on recognition and flattery. And you'll find he'll reciprocate if he hasn't been.*

"*And for God's sake, when you screw up, make a mistake, or blow up for whatever reason—especially when you're wrong—apologize. Apologize. Apologize. There's nothing I know of that builds or mends an ego better than a sincere apology for a righteous wrong . . .*

"*If you're wrong, admit it, compromise and move on. Marriage is a series of compromises.*"

"It doesn't hurt to try to be infallible. But be vulnerable. It will make him feel important to commiserate with you," Marilyn continued.

"If you've made the right choice in the first place, you should have a guy who meets most of your qualifications—he's kind, considerate, thoughtful, honest, has mutual interests with you and is straightforward.

"Of course, is tall, dark, and handsome. You'll notice I put that last," Marilyn concluded.

"And I think you have to deal with faults, too," observed Norma. "Jerry and I have been sleeping in separate bedrooms for quite a while now."

"Oh?" grinned Jackie. "No time for sex or cuddling? Or just bored?" she questioned.

"No. Jerry snores like a locomotive. He was rattling the pictures off the wall at night, even before he came to bed. I've been telling him for a couple years he should see a doctor . . ."

"And?" asked Marilyn.

"Believe it or not, he did last week. Guess he gets lonesome at night. I know I do.

"He went to a sleep clinic at Mercy Hospital and was diagnosed with obstructive sleep apnea. They said he could try some nasal strips on his nose at night but that he had a serious nasal obstruction better removed by surgery. So he's scheduled for that next week."

"A lot of marriages sit on a teeter-totter with something as simple as a treatment or simple cosmetic surgery," Marilyn observed.

"This is serious surgery," blurted Norma.

"And it can get you guys back together," Marilyn observed quietly.

"Doctors told us that six percent of adult men and women in the United States are afflicted with sleep apnea," Norma reported.

"I believe it," said Jackie. "And what about sex?" she added as an afterthought.

"I think it depends on the couple," said Rosemary. "You just have to work that out. I know. I had five kids."

"Yeah, and then your husband ran away," chortled Rosie.

"He just didn't want to work that hard to support everybody. I know that's why he left," Rosemary responded abrasively.

"Yeah," said Marilyn, "and that's probably one of the most important equations in a successful marriage . . . Find a hard worker and a guy who's responsible enough to support you and a large family if that happens."

"Well, you can plan for that a little bit," said Rosie, a Catholic, "and sometimes you can't. But we planned all three of our kids," she added.

"And remained a good Catholic at all times?" chided Katie, a questioning look on her face.

"You're getting' into religion, Katie," said Rosie reproachfully.

"Sorry."

"I'll put the burgers on the grill," Norma announced, retreating to the kitchen after turning on her patio gas grill.

"And, so, how are your kids, Rosemary?" asked Mollie.

"Just fine. They're all working, got good jobs. The younger ones and the older ones who wanted educations got 'em. So I'm free to do my thing—play golf—and try to make money on my investing."

"And how's that going?" asked Julie.

"You want a technical response or a simple one?" Rosemary asked.

"Get as technical as you want," responded Julie, "because I'm thinking about putting some extra money into things. I still have to work, but I'm having trouble getting a sitter for my little girl. My mom isn't as available as I thought she was going to be."

"Common problem," interrupted Leyria, whose two boys were in high school. "It's the older ones that sometimes are a real problem. You just have to keep track of where they are. My David, who's in ninth grade, especially."

"Younger kids would be a simpler matter," she said expansively.

"Not so," answered Jackie, who manages a childcare center. "Bring your kid over. We'll take care of her. How old is she now?"

"Four. How much?" asked Julie point blank.

"Depends on what you can afford," said Jackie. "We can arrange for your little girl if you bring her to us every morning, or on those mornings you need her taken care of for the full day—for something like a hundred and fifty dollars a week."

"I can split up the week? Sometimes my mom can sit for me—"

"Sure thing. Fifty dollars a full day, 6:30 a.m. to 6:00 p.m., or six dollars an hour for a minimum of three hours. And then there's a hundred-dollar enrollment fee. We have a nurse on hand, and all the staff people are first-aid certified and bonded.

"But you have to be careful in your selection, anywhere you choose," Jackie continued. "Talk to the parents who have kids enrolled for care. See how they're treated. And how is the food there especially.

"What's the turnover of kids at these care centers?" Jackie continued. "Do they have an in-house nurse? How many caregivers per kid are there? What's the ratio? Are the daycare providers professionally licensed? Bonded? And the teachers qualified for pre-school instruction?

"Give me a call. We'll work something out," Jackie concluded.

"Okay. I'll do that. I want to do some checking, but I think we can probably get together," Julie surmised.

"Well, back to investments. If you're still interested or can remember asking," cracked Rosemary at Julie.

"Yes, of course."

"Let's sit," announced Norma, motioning to her two picnic tables at the end of the patio. "Burgers are almost done. We can start on the salad, and I've got some peaches and cream corn on the cob and fresh tomatoes for you all. Pretty good for early July, huh?"

"We can talk investments next time," Rosemary said to Julie out the side of her mouth.

"I'll bring some pamphlets from my broker," she added, rising to sit at the picnic table.

"How'd you get the other picnic table?" asked Margaret.

"Borrowed from a neighbor."

Light banter and neighborhood gossip floated around the tables as the Pickle Club members enjoyed the warm July evening and good food.

And they all quietly ruminated Marilyn's usual wisdom about praising and even flattering their husbands. And being vulnerable sometimes, even if you have to make believe.

CHAPTER XI

DINNER AT ROSIE'S

"How many of you guys have had severe menopausal hot flashes?" asked Jackie.

Several hands went up.

"And night sweats?"

"Mine damn near kill me," Jackie said, leaning forward, her chin resting on clenched fists.

The Pickle Club members were all gathered on Rosie's large wooden patio deck off the big kitchen, overlooking a small valley where Marilyn's home sat on the side of the rolling hill below. They were sipping their drinks from an open bar and munching on individual paper plates with crackers, dip, and peanut shrimp from two large trays in the center of the patio.

Rosie's house is a large, sprawling semi-modern ranch with classic lines and a huge great room. It is well furnished and decorated with classic, studded leather furniture, oak coffee and side tables, beige carpeting, and light brown and gray walls.

Rosie has collected several pieces of Chinese art and sculpture from home furnishing stores and several outstanding pieces of sculpture at garage sales that she regularly attends, like the large classic stone Chinese horse and two foot-high Xi'an Shekou terracotta warriors, hand-carved in wood.

The three bathrooms of the house are tastefully done in tile greens, and the four bedrooms are gauzy, heavy with lace and felt embellishments, with polyester bedspreads and décor pillows. Three of her bedroom sets are stunning cathedral cherry with accents of walnut burl in dark, clear mink brown finish. The fourth set, in Mollie's room, is antique white with lavender velvet throw pillows and chairs.

Rosie has had a single mastectomy. "It hasn't diminished my husband's ardor at all," she says. She wears a plastic bra insert to even up her frontal balance.

Rosie's three children, two boys, and Mollie, are grown, in college and have left the nest.

"I sometimes stand in a cold shower, and I swear it starts steaming when I have a hot flash attack," Jackie pointed out.

"As a matter of fact, I'm having one right now," Jackie explained, her face flushed.

"Well, heaven only knows, hot flashes are only one of several symptoms of menopause," explained Margaret.

"My doctor son, when I contacted him after I first started having mine," she added, "said hot flashes are only a constant reminder of a woman's hormonal changes. You can have vaginal dryness, anxiety, depression, and insomnia . . ."

"I've had all those," Jackie complained, fanning her face.

"Well," Margaret continued, "these only tell you your estrogen production has all but ceased. I've had most of the symptoms, too, and they're certainly anything but pleasant.

"My son referred me to a menopause specialist who told me right off that menopause is not a disease, or even an inevitable transition. It's a condition that requires treatment.

"We've all," Margaret continued, "experienced the side effects of the menopausal symptoms—lack of sex drive, pain during what sex we have, and years of hot flashes and stomach cramps.

"And my doctor says we'll start with estrogen and progesterone replacement—Prempro, Premonin. That should reduce the symptoms, protect against osteoporosis and cardiovascular disease."

"Yeah," said Jackie, "I've had those pills, too." Other heads in the group nodded in agreement. "They help reduce only some of the symptoms of menopause. What is it?—Evista, I think I started with—a multiple estrogen replacement. But that didn't stop all the trouble I was having . . .

"I think it prevents osteoporosis and maybe breast cancer."

"Black Cohash," said Norma. Again several heads nodded.

"One or two pills a day," Norma continued. "It's a natural herbal treatment. This improves or eliminates many of the menopause symptoms: hot flashes, the sweating, vertigo, heart palpitations, tinnitus, irritability, and anxiety," she explained.

"Yeah, I've tried that," said Jackie, "and it seems to help a little. This stuff, my doctor says, produces some estrogen-like activity and reduces the pituitary hormone.

"And one of the best things about Black Cohash is there are no side effects like gastrointestinal disturbance," Norma added. "But I still have an outbreak of hot flashes every once in a while."

"Well, I'm sure," Margaret added. "this stuff works. But I have recurrences too."

"So do I," said Jackie, her face still flushed. "I try other stuff, too, with my doctor's permission, like soy products, some 60 grams at a time. This helps reduce my flushing. And vitamins E and C and herbs like red clove, licorice, and chasteberry . . ."

"My God, you guys. You sound like a drugstore or exotic sections of a supermarket . . . ," Angie said, a little unsympathetic sarcasm in her voice.

"You're too young to know anything about this," Rosie said dramatically.

"I've been your age. You've never been mine. Or the age of most of us. So you have all this to look forward to . . . Pay 'tention.

"How was your date, Angie?" Rosie asked, turning from a pouting Mollie.

"Oh, it was okay. We had dinner at Mondos and then went to a movie," Angie answered. "He's a very good-looking guy but kind of shallow. Just talked about sports and stuff most of the time. I like sports, but not for a whole evening. Even the movie was about baseball . . .

"Anyway, I think I'm pregnant . . . ," Angie announced, folding her arms in front of herself.

The entire group sat stunned for a full fifteen seconds, not knowing what to say, unusual for this group.

"Uh, how's that?" stammered Mollie. "You never called me at all about this . . ."

"I didn't know until yesterday. I'd missed my period. We were fooling around in this guy's hot tub after the movie . . ."

"You mean the sports jock?"

"Yeah."

"You can't get pregnant from 'fooling around' in a hot tub," declared Marilyn.

"I think I am," Angie shot back. "We did it in the hot tub."

"Goddam near impossible," snorted Rosemary. "I should know."

"Have you ever done it in a hot tub?" Angie snapped.

"Hell, no. But ask any doctor, and he'll tell you you can't get it done in a hot tub with that much water swishin' around," Rosemary declared.

"How could the guy keep it up in a hot tub anyway?" Marilyn summed up airily.

"Well, I hope you guys are right—'bout it being an impossibility, that is," Angie said hopefully.

"Now I want to tell you guys about my migraine headaches," Angie added quickly.

"Oh, wow. Another relaxing subject," chirped Marilyn.

"You know, I used to get those awful headaches in my forehead and temples," Angie began. "I'd get half sick to my stomach and go sit in a dark room when they got really bad. Sometimes my vision got clouded and blurry," she said, punctuating her complaints by crossing her eyes and fanning her face.

"Sometimes they'd last for a few hours, sometimes they'd go on for day. So I finally went to a doctor. And he asked all about my symptoms, and he said, 'What you have is classic migraine, I think.'

"So we started with Midrin, Topamax, and then beta-blocker Inderal and Blocaden (for prevention of migraine). Topamax is so damnably expensive, I switched to the others. I can use Depacote, too. I think maybe trying Sansert or Imitrex once in a while. They help too. Some of these are anti-depressants or calcium channel blockers. But even Botax for beauty can help prevent migraines."

"You are better now, right?" said Mollie.

"Oh, yes. I feel much better all around. Some of the stuff I've been taking is expensive, but it works."

"Well, I tell you . . . ," Katie started.

"Let's eat," said Rosie, standing. "I'll bring out some TV trays and we can eat out here. It's so nice." Rosie then wheeled out two carts of trays onto the expansive patio deck and pointed to the kitchen. "It's all there, buffet style," she said, pointing.

"Don't you just love picnic-style dinners?" Rosie exclaimed. "No tablecloths, napkins or centerpiece required. Just food. Right, Norma?"

Norma nodded in enthusiastic agreement.

"How's your golf game, Katie?" asked Marilyn.

"Well, I started to tell you guys—I was having back problems, especially after I had played. I went to a doctor, and he told me, after a thorough exam, it wasn't my back necessarily. Of course, you know the back is the hardest thing on the body to diagnose many times for a lot of people.

"And he told me he was going to send me to the golf pro at the Country Club, would you believe? My doctor's a golfer, too, and said since my pain seemed to be in my lower back, that it might be something else, like my golf swing.

"And I told him I'd just won three straight women's golf championships at the Club. And he said, 'I know that. That's why I'm sending you to the golf pro. Might even lower your score and stop your pain.'

"He said also, in an aside, that half the amateurs and a third of the professional golfers think they have lower back problems. I said, 'Okay, I'll try it.'"

"So what happened? What'd the pro say?" asked Rosemary, also a golfer.

"Well, you won't believe this. The pro told me to go through all my swings and strokes. And he told me he sees this a lot. And he's got a golf rehab program. He's sure it'll work for me.

"Know what he told me?" Katie continued. Heads nodded in an eager anticipation of assessment.

"He said my lead hip is the culprit."

"And I said I didn't know what the hell he was talking about. Then he explained.

"'You're a right-handed hitter, right?'" he said.

I said, "Yes."

"'Well, then you know your left hip muscle is so tight when you drive or swing, it's affecting your game. The torque that should be absorbed by your hip is shifted to your back, forcing it to do more work than it should,' he said. He sent me to a sports therapy center in West Des Moines with some directions for them.

"They took videos of my swings and strokes, and, working with the golf pro, they analyzed my frame-by-frame game strokes that showed I wasn't flexing as much as I should.

"They measured," Katie continued, "my hip flexibility, my upper back and leg muscles flexibility, too.

"They told me I had reverse leg shift, too. That is swinging on the drive and long shots with my weight on the back leg instead of the front leg.

"That, plus a little change of force on my lead hip, some exercises to do, and my pain is gone and my game is better. What do you think of that?" Katie concluded.

"Goddam," breathed Rosemary, "sounds like a friggin' miracle."

"A miracle of medical golf science," added Marilyn.

"Well, I don't want the game to get too scientific," Katie declared.

"How's that, Katie?" asked Marilyn.

"It's still a game for me. I enjoy it as a competitive sport.

"Sure, I like to win. But, you know, a lot of golfers these days are going beyond that. They're using methods that in some aspects are taking the game into almost a science. And that's not fun anymore to compete with these people."

"What do they do?" inquired Rosemary, an ardent but amateur golfer.

"Well, they're playing with titanium-capped clubs, new 'sponge' balls, and GPS Systems . . ."

"GPS Systems?" questioned Rosemary.

"Global Positioning Satellite systems. They have a handheld monitor in their golf carts to read off a satellite mirror numbers on the hole flagpoles to get a distance reading for their shots. On golf courses that have them available. And some even triangulate the positions and distances with several readings. Or divide the area into a quadrant for accuracy. Some executives I've seen, who hate to lose, have associates get triangulations and quadrant readings before the match or game. Especially if they're betting on each hole.

"Most tournaments," Katie continued, "prohibit GPS readings in play, though."

"Goddam," exclaimed Rosemary. "I guess I'm out of date."

"No," retorted Katie. "You just play the game for the fun of it. That's all. Like me.

"You don't see Tiger Woods with a GPS monitor in his hand or hanging off his belt when he plays, do you?" Katie added. "Estimating your green and fairway distances is the fun of the game . . ."

"If you watch a golf game, it's fun. If you play it, it's recreation. If you work at it, it's golf," declared Rosemary.

"Yeah. It's self-flagellation," said Rosie emphatically, who had tried golf and gave up, her bra insert almost always ending up under her armpit after every shot attempt.

"Spell *golf* backwards and get my meaning . . ." she added slowly.

"And speaking of science, do you guys know that some audio companies and medicals are researching and selling 'belly talk'?" Marilyn said quizzically.

"Belly talk?" wondered Tiffany.

"Yeah." Marilyn answered. "Parents-to-be talking through the belly to the fetus to get them a head start on the others still being carried and yet unborn.

"And," Marilyn continued to explain, "a couple of groups are selling prenatal education systems that take fetuses through a 16-week course in rhythmic sounds. Another. Womb-Sound Inc. has soon-to-be parents talking to their fetuses with microphones."

"Good God!" exclaimed Norma, usually quiet and listening. "Really?

"Really. A California obstetrician has a program that parents can talk a detailed conversation to their in-utero fetus to simulate their thinking. Medical research has proven that unborns hear and recognize their mothers' voices. But the effect of playing music or trying to teach an unborn phonics is still in doubt," Marilyn added.

"Well, I've heard that women into yoga have doubts, too, about the real value of talking to unborns and playing music for them," said Margaret.

"But they say it makes *them* feel good while they're doing it."

"That's the answer," breathed Norma, standing to stretch.

"Well, I know fetuses respond to external stimuli," Marilyn pointed out. "Just before my daughter was born, I was lying in bed, quietly smoking a cigarette one night. Hubby was out of town, *and she kicked the ashtray off my belly. Was she trying to tell me something?*"

CHAPTER XII

DINNER AT LEYRIA'S

Leyria's home is set on the escarpment of a large, corner lot in a fashionable section of West Des Moines. A large, shuttered ranch-style aqua and cream in color, Leyria's home has a trendy, slim brick facing for the front and inside outer walls, and a triple garage. One for her car, one for her husband, the judge, and one for her two high-school student sons' motorbikes.

Leyria is an attractive, tall, well-proportioned brunette of 41, large brown eyes under shapely, well-contoured brows, a finely sculptured nose, and a generously shaped mouth. She has been a member of the Pickle Club for a year, having been admitted shortly before Tiffany.

Leyria is serving 16% mulled, sherry wine to the Pickle Club on her large, shaded patio this early, warm September evening. The group relaxes on several lawn and beach chairs.

"This is very good," murmurs Jackie appreciatively, holding up her glass. "Sherry?"

"Yep," answers Leyria evenly. "I was sure you'd like it."

"We didn't get to talk about investments at our last two dinners, so I'm glad you called to tell me you were bringing some brochures with you tonight about investing," Jackie said to Rosemary.

"And here they are," Rosemary answered, digging them out of her purse. "My broker's stuff . . ."

"You said the economy was 'ripe' now for investments maybe."

"Yes. U.S. gross domestic product has been increasing at a 3.4 rate for the first two quarters of this year," Rosemary started. "How technical do you want me to get?"

"Much as necessary," Jackie replied eagerly.

"I'm thinking of putting a few extra dollars into investments, too," Leyria added.

"Well," Rosemary began, "that gross domestic product amounts to over an eleven trillion dollar increase in GDP annually adjusted for inflation, which has been running at only about one percent. Big-ticket buys for cars and hard goods is up over eight percent, and unemployment has dropped to five percent. That's a four-year low. So I've been buying more blue-chip stocks in hard goods manufacturing," Rosemary continued.

"Is that all you've been putting money into?" questioned Julie.

"Oh, my, no. I've got a lot of my cash in indexed annuities. You can't get hurt with these," replied Rosemary. "They're indexed to the Dow Standard & Poor's and the NASDAQ Composite Indices. Some are indexed to the Consumer Price Index, too," Rosemary added, "which is up only 2.5%."

"The fixed return goes up or down a little with these indexed annuities, but with the floor they can't go below, so they're fairly safe. I'm buying more.

"How about you, Margaret?" asked Rosemary, knowing that she was also heavily invested.

"Well, I think gasoline prices are abominable. They are so high, a number of my employees are canceling their vacations to go anywhere."

"We've just taken over the second-largest oil-producing country in the world, Iraq, and yet we're paying nearly $3 a gallon for premium gasoline . . . You tell me what's happening," Margaret added.

"I think most of it is our dependence on foreign oil. Remember when it was $49 a barrel for crude? Now it's almost $67," replied Rosemary, frowning.

Angie yawned, Mollie caught it, and both rose to get another glass of mulled sherry.

"What I'm getting at," Margaret continued, "is more ethanol plants for Iowa. And biodiesel fuel processing plants, making diesel fuel from soybeans and animal fats.

"We've got to get more into synthetic fuels," Margaret added, "and wind turbines for energy. And open up Alaska for oil exploration. We all know it's there."

"Renewable energy is the real answer to our dependence on fossil fuels. And to our state's economic growth," Margaret pointed out, gesturing for emphasis.

"I'm not only heavily investing in this area, I'm even toying with the idea of building a couple of ethanol plants."

"Tell me more," Rosemary said eagerly.

"Well, for starters, the U.S. Congress has just approved a bill requiring the use of eight billion gallons of renewable fuel, such as ethanol and biodiesel fuel, annually by 2012, giving fairly good tax breaks on each gallon sold.

"And, by the way, I think ethanol and biodiesel fuels and wind turbines are big time in our state's economic future," Margaret continued.

"No longer can we just rely on agriculture's usual production, manufacturing, insurance, and even gambling to fuel our state's economy, although gambling has certainly helped.

"The fifth 20% of income has to come from renewable energy.

"Iowa's corn growers stand to gain a lot, of course, but think about the environment: Ethanol lowers carbon monoxide emissions as much as 30% and reduces greenhouse gases that contribute to global warming by some 45%," Margaret continued.

Mollie and Angie returned to the attentive group with refills of sherry in hand and tried to follow the intense discussion.

"Is anybody against all this?" questioned Marilyn.

"Well," Margaret continued, "as a manufacturer, I always have to think in scientific, but marketable and energy-efficient terms. Critics say it takes much more energy to produce ethanol than gasoline.

"They're very wrong. It's gasoline refining that results in an energy deficit, returning just 85 BTUs of energy for every 100 BTUs in production. Ethanol, for every 100 BTUs expended in production, returns 165 BTUs of energy. At a 67% overhead cost level."

"How much are we in Iowa already doing in ethanol and biodiesel production?" asked Marilyn.

"I think these figures are close," Margaret replied.

"There are some 25 ethanol plants in Iowa, making high-octane ethanol, high-protein distiller's grain and carbon dioxide. These use up only about 18% of Iowa's corn crop.

"With new biodiesel plants underway in Iowa, distilling soybeans and animal fats, the renewable energy field, including ethanol plants, is growing exponentially. It provides well over $3 billion dollars in economic activity, provides 5,000 jobs and an additional $2 billion dollars in purchases from local suppliers.

"I would say, generally, that research also shows that ethanol could be made from cellulose components of cornstalks, even straw . . . ," Margaret concluded.

"How many biodiesel plants are there now in Iowa?" queried Jackie. "And for heaven's sake, you sound like an encyclopedia on this subject."

"Four," Margaret answered. "I have all this stuff on my desk at the plant now," Margaret added. "That's why I'm so current on this stuff.

"Iowa leads the nation in ethanol production. I'm not only investing heavily but thinking of possibly opening an ethanol-biodiesel distilling plant of my own, getting permits for both," Margaret emphasized.

"Think of it. Just one phase. If we took only a ton of cornstalks from every acre of Iowa's 13 million acres of corn ground and converted it to ethanol, we could still produce a billion gallons and still have enough stalks in the ground to maintain the soil," Margaret pointed out.

"You still own your farm, don't you?" asked Leyria.

"Yes. I still have my 1300 acres in Marshall County. Nearly all of it in corn," Margaret said sheepishly.

"You don't have to apologize for being an entrepreneur," Marilyn said. "If we had your resources, we'd spread them around, too."

"Besides," she added, "what you've got will take care of you in your old age—and provide a nice legacy for your boys when you pass on," she said.

Margaret just smiled and said, "Yeah, right."

"And by the way," Marilyn added, grinning, "there are advantages to growing older. Clothes you buy now won't wear out. Your joints are more accurate than the National Weather Service. And your secrets are safe with your friends, 'cause they can't remember them either."

"Yo," agreed Angie, "and you can live without sex but not without glasses. Right, Marilyn?"

"Ain't that the truth," mumbled Rosie, getting up to get her buffet dinner ready.

"And, incidentally, who the hell ever thought of making biodiesel fuel out of soybeans?" queried Mollie, never expecting an answer.

"George Washington Carver, a poor, black botanist from the South, who did his research on soy and peanuts for biodiesel fuel-making at Iowa State College, as the University was known then," answered Margaret promptly.

"God, you know everything, don't you, Margaret?" joked Marilyn.

"Accumulates with my age, I guess," Margaret replied evenly. "I even sing along with elevator music now after leaving my eye doctor's office, thinking, at my age my eyes can't get any worse."

"Dinner's on. Help yourselves," announced Leyria.

They all stood, stretched, made their potty stops and trooped into Leyria's big dining room for a sit-down roast beef and mashed potatoes-gravy buffet with ice cream and cake dessert. Table conversation covered neighborhood gossip, as it did many times—who was gambling at the racetrack casino too much, and losing, who appeared on the growing bankruptcy filing list in *The Des Moines Register*, who they thought was having an affair, where to buy stretch pants, cut-rate blouses, jackets, and shirts at the best prices—and individual menstrual problems.

Mollie and Angie asked and contributed quite a bit on this one with Tampax versus Kotex (Indian women sat on moss for five days for their periods, Mollie reported), cramps treatment, the pill versus rhythm cycles; intimate, subdued conversations.

Finally, Jackie blurted out, "What do you do for a sagging, loose vagina? Alum baths? Or what?"

Pickle Club members looked at one another in bemused silence for a full ten seconds.

Finally, Marilyn purred, "See your doctor . . . In your case it might take surgery."

CHAPTER XIII

Dating After Sixty

Still at Leyria's home after dinner, while a couple Pickle Club members smoked, others puttered with their ice cream and cake dessert, the conversations switched somehow to dating.

The younger girls, Mollie and Angie, expressed their likes and dislikes about dating younger men.

"Pretty much vanilla," thought Marilyn. Somehow this all sounded familiar to her. The problems of dating in the 20—to 28-year range were basically all the same—cat-and-mouse games of display, replay, and foreplay.

"But what about dating after sixty, Margaret?" Marilyn asked.

"I'm sure you've had some interesting experiences. And I'm also sure you've got a mature point of view now about dating. What do you say about it?"

Margaret sat back in her chair, took a deep breath and said, "Well, I'll tell you all, dating after sixty is a whole new life experience.

"Today, dating for any woman after sixty is so different. With Cialis and Viagra, first of all, it's kind of funny.

"After the date of cocktails and dinner or a show, the guy says, 'Excuse me. I have to go to the bathroom.' You know he's taking a pill. Or, you observe him during the dinner, fumbling in his pockets to make sure he's got his pills with him. And you can usually tell by his facial expressions if he thinks he might get lucky.

"With the guy after sixty, it's mostly all chemical. With the woman, it'll always work. And she can lay there, stare at the ceiling and redecorate her bedroom, wondering if the new curtains she ordered will match her bedspread, while the guy is pumping away, wondering if the ad or his doctor said his erection would last for four hours or four minutes.

"When a woman's dating," Margaret continued, "you can have a good relationship by just being close, and not being intimate necessarily. Without the sex. Because after sixty it's all different anyway.

"After sixty you have to accept where you are. Don't sit and rot away," Margaret continued.

"A woman has to be active after sixty, capture every moment. Keep healthy, try new experiences. Not only to keep in top shape physically but mentally—but to keep alive emotionally, too.

"Never look back. Always look forward."

"Well, that's good philosophy," said Marilyn. "But true and funny, too. What are other differences you've noticed?" Marilyn asked.

"Well, different dating after sixty," Margaret began. " . . . depends on whether you're divorced or widowed.

"If you're widowed, it's all over. If you're divorced, it never ends. At family dinners, both of the partners can't be invited to the event at the same time. This applies either to family or holiday dinners or just get-togethers. It's embarrassing at times.

"And if there's alimony involved, it's really never over. It goes on and on.

"Most men are looking for a nurse or a purse," Margaret continued.

"They think that if you're divorced, you're easy. And if you date a guy who's recently divorced, he's likely to go back to his wife. As I've had happen.

"And as for the widower dates, you know they're always comparing you to their deceased wives. And that's hard to compete with.

"I met and dated one guy who said he was divorced. But I soon found out he was still married. A doctor I dated was just on the make.

"Women lie about their weight," Margaret continued. "Men lie about their income and their age.

"Sex is intimacy to the highest degree. Intimacy has always been a private thing, but this is no longer the case. Sometimes, divorced or widowed women like to flaunt their intimacy with friends or even in public by holding hands and in other ways.

"One area one has to really consider carefully in dating, especially after sixty, is finance. If you're dating, dinners and trips should be shared occasionally. But many single or widowed men are looking for someone to support them.

"In any divorce, it takes two people.

"I've had two husbands of 22 years each. Did I love them? Yes. Both of them . . . at first.

"In my first marriage I was very ambitious and I made all the decisions. In the second marriage, my husband didn't like my success. As an achiever, I was competition for him.

"But back to dating after sixty. How does a woman of sixty get a date? Well, if you're not asked—and often after sixty that's frequently the case—there are a lot of local dating services, Internet dating services, church groups, organizations, friends.

"In any relationship, especially after sixty, the guy wants to be in charge. And what part does honesty play in dating after sixty? You have to be what you are, even when you're dating. You can't posture. You have to be true to yourself. And to your date.

"Her children enter into the equation for the dating woman, especially after sixty," Margaret continued. "And in an important fashion. Even as adults, two of my sons say, 'Why are you dating?' The other says, 'Go for it.' The fourth frowns a lot.

"It's companionship, too, that's important in dating after sixty. There's a difference between dating and just having friends of the opposite sex. To date effectively, you must be yourself at all times, and you can still be interesting and be yourself and still be friends with a guy."

"Well, after sixty, you have the freedom to try new experiences—and dating certainly is one of them," Rosemary observed. "What do you look for in a date after sixty?" she asked.

"Well," Margaret answered, wincing just a little, "that's up to the individual. Some like 'em younger. I like 'em my age, or close to it. And of course financially independent, hopefully handsome in their aging years, and healthy, with more good habits than bad.

"But what the hell. First of all, I'm glad they asked me. Because being asked for a date after sixty *is* an ego trip," Margaret concluded.

CHAPTER XIV

DINNER AT WANG HO'S
MARILYN IS AILING

The hot days of late Indian summer crept into warm days and cooler autumn nights. October's Pickle Club dinner meeting was held at Wang Ho's Chinese Restaurant in the Normandy Terrace of West Des Moines. Marilyn had called to say she wasn't feeling well and could not attend.

It was a strangely subdued group that tried hard to laugh, even when Rosie told Marilyn's railroad switchman's joke (she told her to) as they sipped their drinks.

"Now, sir, you've applied for a job as a switchman. What would you do if you saw two trains approaching each other on the same track?"

"I'd throw the lever and switch one onto another track."

"And if the lever was jammed?"

"I'd turn the signals to red by hand."

"And if the signals were jammed?"

"I'd grab a red flag and run out on the track."

"And if the engineers didn't see you?"

"Aw, shit, man, I'd send for my sister."

"Your sister? What could she do?"

"Nothing, but she loves to watch train wrecks."

"Nothing seriously wrong with Marilyn, I hope," volunteered Katie.

"She didn't say," said Rosie, "when she called, what the problem was. She's been having some bronchial problems."

"Well, it sure is a lot different here without her . . . ," sighed Katie.

"Tell me about it," responded Margaret. "I'm just sorry she can't be here to hear the good news about Tiffany and my son Mark. They're dating . . . I'll have to call Marilyn and tell her, 'cause she's the one, Tiffany, who said we should have you in our club," Margaret explained, turning to Tiffany. Tell 'em about Mark," she directed.

Tiffany brightened as she began. "He's such a wonderful guy. He called me after our last dinner meeting at Leyria's home. Said his mother spoke highly of me, and he asked me out.

"We went out for dinner and a stage performance of pianist Laurie Little and her orchestra at the Civic Center. And then out to the Court Avenue District close by for nightcaps at a couple of bistros there, Trattoria, I think, and the Pub.

"We each tried a Melon Martini and a Pineapple Upside Down . . ."

"What in the world are those?" asked Angie.

"Melon vodka and watermelon pucker, with sweet and sour sierra mist; and Coco rum, pineapple juice, and grenadine respectively," explained Tiffany politely. "We both liked them.

"We had a great time. He's so good-looking."

"How old is he, Margaret?" asked Angie.

"Twenty-five."

"A journalism grad of Drake University, too," added Tiffany. "And so personable."

"Now my vice president for marketing for the company," Margaret pointed out. "He's had a couple years' newspaper reporting experience, and a couple in public relations and marketing for a Des Moines advertising agency. I wanted him to be well-grounded with some practical experience before I took him into the company . . . He's doing a good job. I keep reminding him he's being overpaid . . . ," Margaret slowly added, smiling.

"Well, he said you really gave me a great build-up," continued Tiffany. "He said that you told him how well I play the piano. Said he couldn't wait to hear me play. And, he said," Tiffany added, drawing her shoulders up under a pensive frown, "my beauty was 'breathtaking . . . 'I've never really thought of it quite that way, but he seemed impressed enough. I told him I'd give him a private recital at my place along with some cinnamon-spiced apple cider with a little rum, and maybe even cook a light supper for him.

"We did that a couple weeks ago. He liked my grilled cheese sandwiches with tomato soup and Irish salad and cupcakes I had made along with some ice cream and chocolate.

"We made love right there in the front room."

"Did he use a condom?" snapped Margaret.

"Of course," responded Tiffany. "I also told him about my unfortunate episodes at Vassar and later in New York . . ."

"What did he say about that?" questioned Margaret pointedly. "I didn't tell him about that part of your life."

"He said, 'That's all right.' He said what happened was, to him, understandable but unfortunate but that it certainly didn't really matter."

"And that was it?" demanded Rosemary, one of Tiffany's doubters from the beginning.

"Yes."

"Well, all he told me was that he found you very attractive and seductive," said Margaret dryly as their Korean waiter began distributing their ordered Chinese dinners to their joined tables.

"Since our first dates we've talked a lot by phone. He calls me every day," Tiffany explained. "We talk about his office work, my job at the Library, the movies and plays we've just seen.

"And the books we've both just read or are reading. I have access to the books the Library gets almost every week from publishers.

"We've found we have many favorite authors in common.

"I told Mark I read all these, plus a number of books by authors suggested to me by you guys in the Pickle Club—like James Cain, John Hershey, James Street, Raymond Chandler, William Faulkner, Joseph Wambaugh, Mark Twain, O'Henry, Guy de Maupassant, Ernest Hemingway, Sidney Sheldon, Irving Stone, Elmore Leonard, James Thurber, and Jack London.

"Have I forgotten all those great lady authors of today? Certainly not. I'm reading two of their books now—Danielle Steel, Amy Tan, Joyce Carole Oates, Eudora Welty.

"And, I have to say," Tiffany continued, "wouldn't it be great if we could get some of today's really great historical writers, like David McCullough, Edmond Morris, Bruce Chadwick, Willard Sterne Randall, and John Ensor Harr—to write the history books for today's kids?

"Yeah," she said Mark agreed. "He said he could remember too well the dull, thin-paged, two-inch thick history books he had to wade through in grade school and high school classes.

"He said these guys I just mentioned as great history writers are not only great writers but great researchers who can take the cobwebs out of history and make it all come alive . . .

"Just one more thing," Tiffany said slowly to the intensely interested group, waiting for the waiter to finish taking their plates, she added, "Mark said he wanted me to get a total physical exam with a complete blood workup.

"I told him I had done just that and would show him printouts of the perfectly clear results."

"Hot damn!" exalted Katie. "Looks like you guys are headed somewhere."

"I hope so," said Tiffany, smiling brightly.

"Me, too, actually," concluded Margaret, an optimistic level in her voice.

"I can't wait to call Marilyn to tell her about this. I know she'll be excited," said Katie. "And I want to tell her that my kid has settled down and is doing very well taking bass violin lessons."

And Katie did call Marilyn to tell her as soon as she got home that evening. But first, she wanted to know how Marilyn was doing. What was wrong, and could she help in any way.

"No," said Marilyn hoarsely. "I'm fighting this bronchial thing with antibiotics. I just don't feel well. X-rays aren't showing much except some congestion."

But Katie could almost feel the uplift over the phone when she told Marilyn about Tiffany and Mark, their dates, and their sparking romance. And about her son Bobby doing so well in his music lessons.

"Oh, that's so wonderful," Marilyn remarked. "Mark is a nice guy. Good looking. Smart. Got a great job in the family firm. I'm so happy for him and Tiffany. And I'm happy for you and Cliff—and Bobby.

"As for Tiffany, I don't think she could have done better. He's just a little older than she, but not that much. I think this will develop into a real something for them both," said Marilyn, concluding her phone interview with Katie.

"Oh, yeah. The Pickle Club—and Margaret—will see to that," Katie said emphatically.

Katie related all this to the Pickle Club members at their present gathering.

"Hey, forgot to tell you what a beautiful home you have, Leyria," said Rosie.

"Yeah, great," echoed Mollie.

"Thank you. I'm pretty proud of our décor. We had a lot of help from a decorator, though, with the colors and fabrics.

"I so wanted to create a nice study for the judge. He likes to get away in total silence to review his cases when he can. And I think we got that done," explained Leyria.

"What's he doing lately—the cases? Or can you tell?" asked Rosie.

"Well, what he does is interstate commerce review and comment. These are pretty routine," Leyria explained.

"He gets into racial prejudice hearings and some criminal cases for federal prosecution, and he recently reviewed some eminent domain issues. He doesn't talk to me much about these. Says he shouldn't.

"But one injunction he recently granted," Leyria continued, "was against a printer's union at one of our biggest publishers in town—a cease and desist bench order against those union people putting pregnant women on their picket lines during a recent strike.

"They were even carrying babies, some of them. When the Company's Director of Manufacturing called, with their company's lawyers on the line—sort of a conference call—he invited the judge to come and take a look at this appalling sight. The judge drove over there and said it was one of the most ridiculous things he'd ever seen. Said he'd probably even set a legal precedent. But he promptly issued a cease and desist order, citing a danger to the pregnant women's health, and those carrying babies—to the babies' health, even if they were in carriages. But some of them were just being carried for effect.

"Of course, I'm sure you have all seen the picket line pictures in *The Des Moines Register*.

"But you didn't hear too much about the order the judge gave them. They just quietly pulled *all* the women off the picket lines," Leyria concluded.

"And by the way, Norma, the judge really liked those fudge bars you baked for him. We had them together with our coffee for dessert last night. He thinks that's a great tradition that we have, that the hostess of the dinner sends goodies home for the husband of the month," Leyria added.

CHAPTER XV

DINNER AT JACKIE'S
MARILYN'S DIAGNOSIS CONFIRMED

Each member of the Pickle Club gathered at Jackie's condominium for their November get-together, was handed a cup and saucer of buttered apple grog after doffing their coats and sitting down.

"This is really good," exclaimed Angie, nodding to her cup. "What's in it, Jackie? You're such a connoisseur . . ."

"Gourmet," corrected Mollie.

"Whatever," countered Angie.

"Well, I heated apple brandy—double dosage—vermouth, apple juice and cloves until hot but not boiling. And then I sliced baked apples with butter and a little lemon slice in each.

"You can add maple syrup, which I did, and I stirred 'til the butter melted."

"In each one?" asked Mollie.

"Yes."

"What do you call them?" asked Angie. "They're really good."

"Jackie's Jump," answered Jackie with a prideful smile.

"Well, they're really good," repeated Angie. "You went to a lot of work to put these together one by one. I hope I can have several to kill pain with enough brandy . . ."

"Pain. You sick or what?" asked Jackie.

"Oh, my period just started. And they kill me every time."

"Oh?"

"You're not pregnant then, I hope," murmured Rosie anxiously.

No one had mentioned Angie's announced pregnancy issue before, for fear of embarrassing her.

"No, I'm not, obviously," Angie reported awkwardly.

"And, yeah, a lot of times I get a migraine first as my period starts. My doctor gives me Midrin. He also gave me Inderal to take before my period to prevent the migraine. Most of the time it works. Sometimes it doesn't."

"Didn't your mother give you any secrets about dealing with your periods?" asked Mollie.

"She said a period is a dot at the end of the sentence, and there I am with spots in my panties, and I'm twelve. 'We'll get you some pads,' was all she said. And so I started with Kotex.

"But my dad was nicer. Said I was a young woman now, and he had sent me a nice card with four roses: red for love, yellow for friendship, pink for happiness, and white for purity."

"That's really sweet," said Rosie.

"Well, traditional treatments be hanged," snorted Rosemary.

"With all the new, good drugs to take for menstrual pain and cramps, who wants ice or herb packs . . . ?"

"Exactly, Rosemary," responded Angie.

"My doctor has prescribed Motrin, Midol, Advil, or ibuprofen," Angie began. "Whatever works best for me. So far it's been Motrin and Midol that work for me for cramps. This brandy stuff should help, too. I may still hurt, but I won't give a damn."

There was a lull in the conversation as the group breathed in the vapor of their drinks and sipped them.

"I wonder where Marilyn is," Rosemary said matter-of-factly.

There was a long silence. And then Katie delivered the saddening, stunning news.

"She's not coming. Possibly not ever again." Then she broke down and cried. Sobbing, she added, "Marilyn's husband called me—from the hospital—to tell me she's got terminal cancer."

There was a deafening silence as each of the Pickle Club members looked at one another in disbelief.

"Oh, my God," said Jackie as the group retreated into another emotionally chilling, numbed silence.

Finally, recovering somewhat, Katie stammered, "I don't know how any of us can live without her being around. She's my second mother."

Even though Katie made the 24-hour flight to Seoul, Korea, stopping on the way in Honolulu about every other year to see her sister and her family, she made the long trip especially to see her aging mother. But it was Marilyn who taught Katie how to crochet and how to sew and tell the difference between a running stitch, overcast stitch, and a blind stitch; how to pleat a blouse, hem a skirt, and dart a jacket.

"Well, we'll all make it. We did after Nancy and Mary passed on from the Pickle Club," said hard-hearted Rosemary emphatically, who, like a neutered beagle, seldom showed any emotion.

"Yeah, but we had Marilyn to help us through those tough times," sniffled Katie.

"What the hell happened?" asked Rosie. "She didn't tell me she had anything serious."

"She didn't know," replied Katie, "until just yesterday. She went to her doctor who had been taking chest x-rays, but the congestion didn't seem to be clearing up, so he ordered a CAT scan," Katie continued. "Marilyn's husband tells me her doctor then told her the CAT scan and biopsy showed a malignant growth from the upper portion of her right lung to the base of the esophagus.

"Inoperable, he said. The cancer was *behind* the congestion which showed in the x-rays."

"Goddam," sighed Rosie. "Sonofabitch. There goes another one. And I'm not trying to be funny. What are they doing for her?"

"Well, Don says they've got her on oxygen and morphine. And they're starting her on chemotherapy tomorrow. He says, optimistically, it's manageable but incurable. Marilyn's daughter is flying in tonight from New York to be with her. That's about all I know. Here is her room and phone number at the Younkers Wing of Iowa Methodist Medical Center," Katie offered.

"But that'll probably change from time to time; if it does, they'll tell you where she is."

"How long has she got?" questioned an anxious Angie, her menstrual pain forgotten.

"Well, they think three to six months."

"Visitors?"

"Sure. Anytime," Katie said, a little reassuring.

"Marilyn's husband saw to it that she got a nice room with a view and the best doctors."

Flowers and cards flowed into Marilyn's room as her stay lengthened to ten days while undergoing her first chemotherapy treatments. She'll get to go home for the holidays—Thanksgiving and Christmas—coming back to continue the weekly Lab tests and chemotherapy at the John Stoddard Cancer Center, a five-story treatment section of Iowa Methodist Medical Center.

* * *

Lab tests, with complete blood workups, are all done weekly for Marilyn in late November and early December, on the first floor of the John Stoddard Cancer Center.

Chemotherapy is administered on the fifth floor. A huge, brightly lighted room with individual chemo intravenous feeding stations arranged in a gigantic horseshoe shape around the room. Each is comfortably furnished with a lamp, reclining chair, and endtable with Kleenex, mints, and magazines neatly arranged on each. A second recliner chair sits on the opposite side of each endtable for a companion or nurse to sit.

Behind the counter move the energetic nurses and confident administering technicians. At one end of the huge counter is a laboratory running the entire width of the room, where doctors and nurses ponder current tests and procedures.

Marilyn was painlessly confident and happy with her treatments. But she has visited the fourth-floor "bonnet" room where chemotherapy patients can select a dress knit cap or hat or a fashionable baseball of their choice as their hair begins to fall out from the chemotherapy treatments.

Marilyn prepared her Christmas cards early, with individual notes on each, as usual, but she added the following insert to each as they were mailed:

> Dearest friends,
>
> Having just been diagnosed with lung cancer, and having already finished the Christmas cards, I decided to drop a note to tell you. It's not curable, but manageable. I've started chemotherapy in late November and will go from there. I am not mourning my life but celebrating it! I want to go out as my little and youngest friend calls me, "Laughing Marilyn."
>
> Apprehensive? Yes. Scared? No. I have a wonderful support system from the past generation in my wonderful husband and children, not to mention those surrounding me each and every day, everywhere, forever!
>
> Painful? Not yet. And I have lots of strong medicines around to help.
>
> My curiosity sometimes gets the best of me, because of the unknown. You can ask me anything, and as long as my brain goes on, I'll tell you.
>
> See ya later.
>
> Love,
> Marilyn

Family, friends, and relatives all come to the hospital to host individual Thanksgiving and Christmas parties for her in the large visitors' lobby on her room's floor. Marilyn's son Jamie entertains his mother and out-of-town guests at his home for Thanksgiving.

After arriving home, Marilyn is still mobile but tiring easily.

The doctors have done bone imaging of Marilyn's whole body, and CAT scans of her head and brain with dye. They begin the Darbepoctin alfa injections with Carboplatin and Etopisid and saline. Etoponde and

Dexamethanone follow. There are extremity studies, electrocardiograms, Doppler-echo heart tests.

Marilyn attends her son's office Christmas party at the Des Moines Golf and Country Club in a wheelchair. And has a good time. But she's failing fast. Her wedding rings keep slipping off her fingers, and her coordination is diminishing.

CAT scans with dye of her thorax and abdomen and other tests, including a deep biopsy, show the cancer has spread to her liver. Her body potassium levels drop precariously low, and she has to begin taking two tablespoons of raw liquid potassium each night, along with 4 to 6 milligrams of liquid morphine.

Family cousins begin coming in from Denver, Bella Vista, Arkansas, and Finley, Ohio, to pay their last respects just before Marilyn is readmitted to Iowa Methodist Medical Center in early January to go on oxygen and continuous intravenous feeding.

The Pickle Club has a special Christmas party for her, her family and grandchildren, in her commodious suite at the hospital. Gifts are exchanged and tearful sentiments expressed.

Everyone knows this is the "dying room," a large, well-lighted room with three recliner chairs, two endtables and a floor lamp.

Marilyn's daughter has a foldaway cot brought into the room and begins staying all night with her. Marilyn's team of doctors begins radiation treatments, and she undergoes surgery to enlarge her esophagus with stents.

Medical consultants are brought in to discuss with Marilyn's husband, son and daughter, upcoming procedures, as they agree on no extra heroic, life-lengthening measures to be taken as Marilyn begins to fail, her blood oxygen levels and vital signs rapidly deteriorating.

In one of her last cognitive acts, Marilyn writes the following to be mailed to her Christmas card list by her husband:

> *Dear Family and Friends,*
> *I have come to the end of my road.*
> *And the sun has set for me.*
> *I like no nights in this gloom-filled room.*
> *Why cry for a soul set free?*
> *Miss me a little, but not too long.*
> *And not with your head bowed low.*
> *Remember the love that we once shared.*
> *Miss me . . . but let me go.*
> *For this is a journey that we all must take,*
> *And each must go alone.*

It's all a part of the Master's plan,
A step on the road to home.
When you are lonely and sick of heart,
Go to the friends we know,
And bury your sorrow in doing deeds.
Miss me . . . but let me go.

Love,
Marilyn

CHAPTER XVI

─────────

MARILYN'S JOURNEY HOME

Marilyn made a special effort to be alert on a cold, mid-January afternoon for a visit from Margaret, Tiffany, and her new beau, Mark.

Marilyn spoke hoarsely, but warmly, of how glad she was that Tiffany and Mark had gotten together.

"And we are getting married in May," Tiffany announced, showing Marilyn her emerald-cut diamond engagement ring Mark had just given her.

"You're the first to know."

"I'm so happy!" Tiffany exclaimed, turning to Mark with a warm kiss.

"I know you two will be great together," Marilyn murmured slowly.

And turning her eyes to Margaret, she slowly added, "And, thank you, dear Margaret, for your cards, flowers, your friendship—and for this," nodding towards Tiffany and Mark.

"Yes. Thank you. You're most welcome for all that, Marilyn. I know they'll have a great future together," said Margaret.

"I'm going to build Iowa's largest ethanol plant on the back lot of our manufacturing complex, starting immediately. I'm going to call it, 'Marilyn Place.' And I'm putting Mark in charge of all this to oversee construction and its operation."

"And I'm offering Tiffany her choice," said Mark, "of going to law school at Drake University, one of the best in the country—or having a family. Or both. It's her choice."

"How wonderful," Marilyn murmured, barely audible, moving a pointed finger in an arc toward the happy pair.

"I've learned so much from you Pickle Club guys," Tiffany gasped. "I learned how to love, think, and you all have really built up my self-esteem . . . *I've come to know myself.*

─────────

Yes, Tiffany indeed, felt reborn. Her past, unemotional life had become a distant memory.

Her lack of parental love, frustrating and fleetingly distant—like any youth trying to catch a hummingbird—has been replaced by the love, understanding and caring of the Pickle Club members.

And her first sexual experience by a cold, calculating football jock has become a dim reminder of her vulnerability, like only a broken New Year's resolution, now with Mark's love and affection for her.

"I thank you, Marilyn," Tiffany began, tears brimming in her eyes, her voice trembling, "for all you and the guys in the Pickle Club have done for me, too. But you, especially, Marilyn, because you're the leader, and I probably wouldn't have even gotten in if it hadn't been for you . . . Thank you so much."

Tiffany then shrugged, a questioning expression on her face, as she regained her composure. "I'm going to try to be a good wife," she said slowly, taking her eyes from Mark's to Marilyn, who by now had dozed off. But she was smiling.

At 3 p.m. the next day, her blood oxygen levels dropping, her heart racing and breaths coming in short gasps through the oxygen tubes in her nose, a comatose Marilyn died, her husband, daughter and son holding her hands.

*   *   *

Marilyn's funeral, after the largest visitation crowd in the history of McLaren's Funeral Chapel in West Des Moines, was held at Westminster Presbyterian Church in Des Moines.

In size, the huge Westminster Church is comparable to more than half the size of the center concourse of the Cathedral Church of St. John the Divine on Amsterdam Avenue in New York City, possibly the largest cathedral in the world.

And it was packed. Marilyn's immediate family, friends, relatives, and acquaintances heard her eulogized by the lady pastor, Amy Miracle, as a full-spirited, delightful, charming human being who brought joy, cheer, and many good stories to all who knew her.

But it was the eulogy from Marilyn's Pickle Club friends, read by beauteous Katie, as she stood, resting her hand on Marilyn's casket, in front of the sacristy before the entire assemblage, that brought tears to everyone's eyes:

> *This is heartfelt from Marilyn's Pickle Club friends:*
> *"Marilyn was our friend,*
> *And we love her.*

"We call ourselves
The Pickle Club.

"We had no causes, we challenged nothing.
We talked a lot,
But most of all we laughed a lot.
"The restaurateurs put us in back booths,
As we laughed a lot.

"We took trips to Kansas City—Webster City,
Anyplace anyone wanted to go.
And we laughed a lot over our dinners.

"Marilyn was special to us,
As we knew we were special to her.

"We tried to help her,
But she asked for nothing and never complained.
It was hard to help.
And we still laughed a lot.

"Maybe, Marilyn, we should have called it
The Laughing Club.

"We will not have an empty chair,
As is done for deceased players in orchestras.
But we have empty hearts, though, too.

"Goodbye, dear friend.
We will miss you.
You have taught us much,
And you will be with us always!

"We know that you'll
Get 'em laughing in heaven, Marilyn.
Reserve a table in the rear,
As we're not far behind, dear friend.
And then . . . once again . . . we'll laugh a lot."